Moeller Law Office

424 W. Broadway
Farmington, NM 87401

THE

BODY

IN THE

CORNFLAKES

Also by K. K. Beck

THE
BODY
IN THE
CORNFLAKES

◆

K. K. BECK

St. Martin's Press
New York

Design by Tanya M. Pérez

ISBN 0-312-08146-4

For Oliver Beck, with thanks

1

"Clean-up on aisle three." Ted Constantino flipped off the intercom and sighed. It was bad. Salad oil. As spills went, it was right up there with mayonnaise and peanut butter. From his perch in the office, high above the selling floor, he looked out through the slit of the two-way mirror, and nervously ran a hand over his jaw.

Nobody seemed to be hustling over there with a mop, but a little old lady with a walker, listing slightly because of a heavy nylon shopping bag hanging from one handle, was making steady progress toward the oil slick.

"Damn," said Ted, running out from behind the desk and clattering down the steps, dodging a sawhorse and a

1

sheet of plasterboard on the way down. The poor old thing probably had osteoporosis. Her hips would snap like two dry twigs. At the bottom of the stairs, Ted snagged a yellow plastic sign that said CAUTION: WET FLOOR and bore the silhouette of a falling human being, and pushed through the swinging metal door.

Ted's mind could race along at breakneck speed while he was imagining disaster. As he pushed past floral and deli and huffed up the frozen aisle, careening around an end aisle display of corn chips, Ted's inward eye saw the old lady robbed of her independence, a lonely shut-in. Then he saw a montage of frustrating years of lawyers' depositions, and courtroom battles. He imagined himself leaning intensely forward in the witness stand, explaining how he did his very best to get to aisle three in time. He imagined the store's attorneys pleading with Karl Krogstad to settle. And, he knew what Karl's reply would be. "Everybody wants a free ride. The hell with the old bitch. I'll see her in court."

When he reached aisle three, he managed to interpose himself between the old lady and the salad oil, flipping open his sign and setting it down. He noticed she wore incredibly thick trifocals, so he read the sign to her. "I'm afraid we have a spill here," he said pleasantly, holding out his arm to guide her away.

"What?" she said.

At the end of the aisle, Ted was pleased to see Jason, a muscular young courtesy clerk, with a mop. On closer inspection, however, he realized Jason was leaning on the mop and blushing while a thirtyish brunette woman chatted with him. "I always have trouble getting these jars open," she was saying, holding up a pickle jar. "Now that I'm single again, I sure miss having a man around to get those pickle-jar lids off." She tilted her head to one side and looked up at Jason with the gleam of a statutory rapist.

"Jason!" he barked out. "We got a spill here." He glared

2

at the woman. "Try bulk foods for pickles in plastic containers with snap-on lids," he said coldly.

"But they're not recyclable," said the woman, who followed Jason up the aisle and watched his biceps work as he mopped.

Ted turned his attention to the old lady who was struggling to reach the top row of the salad oil section, her small bird-like hand straining toward a glass bottle of olive oil. Her walker began to tip forward. "Let me help you," said Ted.

"What?" she said as the shopping bag on the walker's handle swung heavily into a row of larger bottles of olive oil. Ted fell to his knees between the walker and the olive oil and managed to extend his arm across the shelf. He held his position until he was sure all the bottles were securely upright.

"Nice save," said Jason approvingly.

"Thanks," said Ted, smiling with relief. As he attempted to stand, however, the old lady shifted her walker to one side, one rubber foot pinning Ted's hand to the floor. Wincing with pain and acting on sheer instinct, he tried to pull it out, tipping the walker, the old lady, and her heavy shopping bag forward.

She slid down the front of the shelf, snagging several quart bottles she had tried to hang on to on the way down.

Horrified, Ted scrambled up and looked down at the crumpled old lady surrounded by a spreading pool of olive oil and shards of glass. Jason grabbed the old lady around the waist and set her upright. "Gentle," said Ted. Jason was maneuvering the old girl like a hundred-pound bag of charcoal briquets. Ted insinuated the walker in front of her and wrapped her white-gloved hands firmly on the handle.

"Are you all right?" he said. "Shall we call a doctor?"

"My son's a doctor," she said. Then she smiled. "My other son's a lawyer."

3

"You must be very proud of them," said Ted, his heart sinking. "Are you sure you're all right?"

"I think so," said the old lady. "My, wasn't that silly of me. I just wanted that little bottle up there." She began to reach again.

"Stop!" shouted Ted, "I'll do it. This one?"

"Why yes, thank you."

Jason and the other woman were on their knees now, collecting all the groceries that had fallen from the old lady's bag. "My, Jason, you're really strong," the brunette said, eyeing the name tag on one of his overdeveloped pecs. "You just picked her right up, didn't you?"

"Jason's awfully developed for a boy his age," said Ted pointedly. "Better get this olive oil cleaned up, guy."

"Wow," said Jason. "Two quarts."

"That's right," said Ted, taking the last of the spilled groceries from the brunette and staring her right in the eye. "Extra-virgin."

Her eyes narrowed and she patted her hair into place and rose. "I saw the whole thing," she said to Ted. To the old lady she added, "Let me give you my name, hon. You might need a witness."

Ted hooked the bag back onto the walker. "You can leave your name at the courtesy desk," he said. "I'll escort this lady to the front end, and we can get someone to finish her shopping for her. Would you like us to send you home in a cab, ma'am? Courtesy of Galaxy Foods, of course. And, today's shopping is on us," he added desperately.

The brunette was looking in her purse for a pen. "You better give your son the attorney my name and number. In case you sue," she said.

"What?" said the old lady.

"Leave your name and number with Jason, there," said Ted. The brunette mulled over this suggestion for the second Ted needed to hustle the old lady away down aisle three.

4

Ted was delighted to see Karen Hamilton coming up aisle seven. Karen, a pretty lady in her late forties with a sweet manner and soft blond hair, was the manager of the floral department and helped choose general merchandise. She was also the owner's daughter, which meant she didn't really have to do anything, but she enjoyed puttering around the store in a benign way, and she had a terrific way with customers.

"Hello Ted," she said with her usual air of surprise. Why she should be surprised, Ted couldn't imagine. He'd been assistant manager here for two years now. "How nice to see you." She was carrying a basket with some small teddy bears in it. "Aren't these cute? I thought we could put them up by the register."

"Good idea," said Ted, imagining whining children in line wearing down their mothers with requests for the heftily marked-up bears. "Listen Karen, this lady just had a little spill."

"Oh no!" Karen looked genuinely alarmed.

"I told her we'd finish her shopping for her, and call her a cab."

"You said my groceries would be free, too," said the old lady.

Great, thought Ted. Now she was probably going to play supermarket sweep. Probably head right for the meat counter and start tossing in hams. Karen gave Ted a startled look that indicated she was thinking along the same lines. Despite her habitual vagueness, she was her father's daughter. Retail to the core.

"I'll take care of everything," said Karen, putting the basket of bears on her arm and leading the old lady away. Ted sighed with relief. Whatever happened now, it happened on a Krogstad's watch.

On his way back to the office, Ted okayed a check, ad-

5

judicated a dispute with a customer about a coupon item, and swung by produce to take a look at the new awnings. The store was going through a major remodeling, and there were banners hanging everywhere reading EXCUSE OUR DUST and WE'RE REMODELING TO SERVE YOU BETTER.

Sales had slumped as the store had been torn up, and the work was three weeks behind schedule. Ted hoped they'd recoup during the upcoming grand reopening and re-model sale, set for two weeks from now. Just today, Karl Krogstad had complained that he was "bleeding to death."

Ted looked critically around the produce area. It looked good. The produce was nicely trimmed and displayed. He nodded at Jimmy, one of the produce guys, who was setting out clipped carrots in an artful manner.

"I see you got the new aprons," he said. Jimmy wore a kelly green apron, designed just for produce, with a perky carrot stenciled on the front. The guys hadn't wanted to wear aprons with pictures on them, but the store decor people had insisted. "Looks nice," said Ted, trying to sound sincere.

Jimmy made a face. "Can't I have one with a bunny?"

"Come on," said Ted. "They're cute. Besides, they're supposed to match the awnings."

He glanced up at the awnings as workmen lifted them into position. To his dismay, he noticed they were a pale yellowish-green. They didn't look anything like the kelly green aprons.

"Damn," he said to himself. "Hey!" he shouted to the workman on the stepladder. "That's not what we ordered."

"The darker green was back ordered," said the man. "Your boss said to substitute."

"Yeah? Who?"

"I don't know. The manager."

Ted sighed. The awnings looked terrible. They were sup-posed to give an old world open air market look to the produce department, but somehow, the light came

6

through the poison green, casting everything in a sickly shade.

"Hang on!" said Ted. "Don't do another thing. Wait."

He turned on his heel to head back for the office and see what he could do to fix the problem.

Before he got out of produce, however, a thin, serious-looking young woman with a pale baby strapped to her back accosted him. Both mother and baby had dark circles under their eyes. Smiling at babies was a part of his job Ted enjoyed, but this specimen was no candidate for a Gerber label. "I want to know what pesticides are used on these products," she said accusingly, cornering him with her cart. "They all look kind of creepy."

Those awnings had to go. Period. Ted was going to raise hell about it.

"Just a trick of the light," said Ted. "Our produce is all just fine. Pesticide levels are all below FDA limits, but we also have an organic produce section." He gestured over his shoulder, planning to duck out before the woman discovered that the organically grown products were smaller and homelier, and started to bitch about that.

The woman leaned suspiciously over the display, just as a mister set off, sending a fine spray of water over the baby on her back.

"Those sprinklers could have deadly disease germs in them!" said the woman hysterically. "I read about that somewhere."

Ted turned around and went back to her side. "We don't use a misting system that recycles the water. There have been problems with systems that have the water in holding tanks, but we don't use those systems," he said, as Jimmy reached for a paper towel and blotted off the child. The kid remained listless and impassive, probably, thought Ted, because of an inadequate diet resulting from food paranoia.

7

"Then aren't you wasting water?" said the woman triumphantly.

Ted sighed. "We thought about it long and hard," he said, "and decided this was the best for our customers." He looked her straight in the eye and said with as much sincerity as he could muster: "We do everything we can to make sure the products we sell are medically, socially, politically, and ecologically correct."

He glanced over at her cart, hoping to see disposable diapers or a carton of cigarettes, or at least a can of tuna that might have figured in the untimely death of an appealing marine mammal, but there was only a plastic bag of lentils from bulk foods and bottled spring water.

She thawed a little. "Have you heard you can get cancer from some of these microwave packages?" she said half-heartedly.

"Our customers aren't all as sophisticated as you are about the buying choices they make," said Ted smoothly, "but we're trying to educate them." She opened her mouth to say something more, but he rolled right over her. "Hey, we know it's a fragile planet. As a matter of fact, we think beyond global. That's why we're called Galaxy Foods." The woman nodded solemnly. "Jimmy, explain to the lady about the advantages of misting the produce, won't you?"

Ted rushed back to the office, hoping to find the manager, Karl Krogstad, Junior, there. Ted checked his watch. It was two. Junior's blood alcohol level should be just about right. Soon enough after lunch for him still to be pleasant, but not too far into the day—that irritable patch after lunch wore off and before the cocktail hour began.

What he found back in the office was a trio of Krogstads. They were surveying the remodeling going on behind the scenes in the pathetic nest of cubbyholes that served as offices. Karl, the patriarch and owner, was expounding on his remodeling philosophy. "The customers don't see it, don't put nothing into it," he said, indicating some ghastly orange-flecked shag carpeting he was having installed over the plywood floors. "And we're getting some extra space by taking in the old catwalk area that used to run along the end of the store. It'll give us a few more feet and it's already framed in pretty good, so we can just throw up some paneling. I got some ceiling tiles left over from when we did the rec room at home."

Karl was a big square-jawed Norwegian with hooded blue eyes and a mouth that was a mean little line. Vigorous and fit, he had thick silver hair, and fierce brows. Ted admired the old man, but he didn't particularly like him. Karl spent a lot of time managing his other investments, having turned over day-to-day store operations to his son— who had always been referred to as Junior—but whenever he felt like it, Karl jerked the leash, and threw in a little humiliation for good measure.

Junior, the store manager, preferred the title "store director." In his late forties, he was softer and puffier than his father, with a patchwork of broken veins that indicated he'd hammered back about a billion bourbons in his time. He looked over the renovations with little more than polite interest. "Good, Dad," he said. His hair was dark blond, shot through with silver, sprayed into a stiff arrangement that made his own hair look like a cheap toupee.

Ted always felt his heart lighten at the sight of Junior's blue Buick Riviera cruising out of the parking lot. Ted found Junior amiable enough, but resented his incompetence. Fortunately, it was accompanied by sloth and drunkenness, which meant Ted had pretty much of a free hand as assistant manager, as long as he worked around Junior tactfully and made sure Junior got credit for everything good that happened.

"Ted! Look who's back!" said Karl, putting his arm around his grandson. Lance was tall, too. Ted, whose family was Italian, always felt small and compact and dark when he was surrounded by these Vikings.

9

"Hi, Lance," said Ted, noting the European silk suit, the slicked-back hair, the scent of powerful cologne, and what appeared to be a large red zit over one eyebrow. Junior's son, Lance, was a college boy in his early twenties. Ted hadn't seen him since last summer, when he'd irritated customers and employees alike, working as the slowest checker in the history of the retail grocery business. He'd shown considerably more energy putting moves on most of the younger females on the staff.

"Lance just graduated," said Karl, beaming with grand-fatherly pride. "From that food management school down there at USC."

The University of Spoiled Children, thought Ted to himself. "Congratulations, Lance," he said. Lance probably minored in Porsche polishing. "Kind of hard to leave that beach, huh? Are you up here in Seattle on a visit?"

"No," said Lance solemnly. "I'm here to put my education to work."

"We're bringing the boy on board," said Junior, sliding behind his desk and putting his feet next to the golf trophy there. "There's gotta be something he can do around here, Ted. You figure it out. Dad—that is, Dad and I—we want him to learn the entire operation, inside and out."

"Well, we're all full up with checkers," lied Ted, remembering what a bottleneck Lance was. "Course we could use an extra courtesy clerk—"

Lance smirked at his grandfather.

"Listen," said Ted, "we got a problem right now we gotta take care of. There's some guys putting up awnings in produce, and they make the produce look really sick. I've had one customer complaint already. We ordered a sort of darkish green, but this stuff looks like bile. We have to stop those guys."

"Eye appeal is everything in this business," said Lance knowledgeably.

"Tell me about it," said Ted heatedly. "Right now the produce looks like hell."

"Produce is a key department," continued Lance, as if by rote. "A store's reputation can rise or fall on perceived produce quality."

"Smart kid," said Karl. "They taught him a bundle."

"And it cost a bundle too," said Junior, chuckling and twirling his diamond pinkie ring.

"Well, let's get those awnings out of here and call the company and get the ones we ordered," said Ted.

"Fine," said Junior vaguely. "That awning salesman called me a couple of days ago. Come to think of it, he did say something about some green fabric."

"I'm not sure awnings are the way to go anyway," said Lance, slipping away from his grandfather and perching on his father's desk. He dangled one foot, clad in a shiny Italian loafer. "Don't you think neon is a little more contemporary?"

"Neon," said Karl thoughtfully. "Lance thinks neon."

Ted knew he was in big trouble.

"Maybe we *can* get you on as a checker, Lance," he said in what he knew was a desperation move. "We've got an opening on nights. Might be good to have you on nights to keep an eye on the night crew. I think we've got a grazing problem." Ted had found some empty Häagen-Dazs containers in the freezer and some empty Michelob bottles stuffed into an end-aisle display of Kraft Macaroni & Cheese dinners.

"Grazing problem!" snapped Karl. "Find out who it is and fire their ass. I won't tolerate anyone stealing from me." His face grew red. "Ted better work a night shift or two this week to work on it."

"Well, I was suggesting Lance might check it out," said Ted. "Seeing as we need to find a slot for him."

Karl waved his hand impatiently. "I don't want him to be

11

a checker. Teach him everything you can about your job. Then we'll find something for him."

Terrific, thought Ted. And what'll you find for me? He looked over at Lance and smiled tightly. "Sure," he said.

"Good," said Karl. To his grandson he said, "Ted's good. He'll tell you everything you need to know."

Ted was tempted right now to tell Lance to stop by the health and beauty aids section, aisle five, and pick up something for that ugly zit over his eyebrow.

"Right," said Lance, sliding from the desk and assuming an alert, eager stance. "Let's tackle that awning problem immediately. I don't want ugly produce in my store."

"Neither do I," said Ted.

2

◆

"Okay Ginger, let's try it again."

Ginger Jessup wet her lips, wrinkled her nose, closed her eyes in a gesture of concentration worthy of Stanislavsky, and opened them up again with an alert expression.

"You look real nice," said Mel for the fourteenth time during the shoot. Ginger seemed to need reassurance.

"Why, thank you, Mel," she said in a girlish voice, and then, on cue, she dropped an octave and added a lot of breath to her delivery.

"Price. Quality. Service. Making sure our customers get it all is what Galaxy Foods is all about." She began pushing a shopping cart slowly toward the camera, and tilted her head to one side, narrowing her eyes thoughtfully. "It just makes me feel good to know Galaxy Foods is a part of my family's life-style—and part of the good life here in the Pacific Northwest." The thoughtful moment over, her lips slid easily into a smile, revealing beautiful white teeth.

"How was that?" said Mel to the camera operator.

"She didn't end up out of frame in that one," he said. Mel, the creative director for the United Independent Grocers advertising department, scrunched next to the cameraman and watched the videotape played back. "Ginger looks great, but those shelves look crummy. Let's face those cans of tomato sauce."

The production assistant, a serious-looking young woman with short dark hair and faded jeans, strode down the aisle and began twirling cans so all the labels looked symmetrical, and Ginger Jessup went and sat down in a canvas chair.

Madge, her makeup artist, a motherly-looking woman with gray shingled hair and wearing a pink smock came and sat in the chair next to her.

"I look bad today. I know I do," said Ginger with a pout.

"No you don't, honey," said Madge, digging in a pocket and coming up with some blusher. "Let's just put a little sparkle on you."

Ginger Jessup was a study in orange—from her carroty red hair, arranged and lacquered in artful disarray, to her tawny skin from the tanning parlor, to her shiny coral mouth. Madge brushed two wings of orange over her cheekbones. Only Ginger's narrow green eyes fringed in charcoal lashes broke up the monochromatic palette.

"That was a terrific reading, Ginger," said Mel, turning away from the soup cans.

"Gosh, thanks, Mel," said Ginger with another wide smile, wriggling a little in her chair, and batting her eyelashes.

"Gosh, thanks, Mel" mouthed the production assistant

silently, with a coquettish grimace as she twirled soup cans.

Mel intercepted the look and went over to the young woman. "Come over here a minute, Janice," he said, leading her out of the bright lights about twenty feet away. "I saw that," he said fiercely, as Janice shifted her weight from one foot to the other and sulked. "We can't alienate the talent. What if she'd seen you imitating her?"

"I'm sorry," said Janice sullenly.

"What's the problem anyway?" demanded Mel in an exasperated whisper.

"She's so awful. She doesn't belong in these spots," said Janice. "She looks like a whore. No one believes she's a shopper."

"I think she looks sweet," said Mel, obviously perplexed. "She really is a nice person."

"Oh God," said Janice.

"Envy is an ugly thing," said Mel in a serious voice.

"I'm not envious. I don't want to be like her. It's just that she's so cheesy. Can't you see it?"

"Look," said Mel, "the grocers love her, she always shows up with her lines memorized, and she looks sweet."

"Jesus," said Janice.

"Yeah, well you'd better be civil, that's all," said Mel. "I expect professionalism on my shoots."

"I mean, she has those ridiculous plastic tits," continued Janice.

"So she's enhanced her breasts a little for proportion's sake," said Mel. "That's show biz,"

"They look like satellite dishes. Does she have to wear that spandex dress?"

"It's a great dress," said Mel. "Let's face it. She's got a great body."

"Okay, okay. Never mind," said Janice, running a hand through her short hair.

"Just throttle back, for God's sake" said Mel.

15

They went back on to the set, and Janice continued her work on the shelves.

"I don't know why I always go for older men," Ginger was saying to Madge. She giggled. "But I know why they go for me. I can always get a rise out of 'em."

Madge gave her a playful push and cackled harshly. "You're so bad," she said.

"No," said Ginger, with a sly smile. "I'm *so-o-o* good."

3

Monday at two o'clock, when he showed up for Krogstad's Galaxy Foods weekly ad meeting, Ted was slightly depressed to see Lance in attendance. Lance was sitting on his father's desk adjusting his tie and turning his toe from side to side admiring the gleam on his Italian loafer.

"Ted, my man," said Lance, not bothering to look up from the hypnotic sight of his shiny shoes.

"Hello, Lance. Haven't seen you around for a few days." Ted had supposed it was too good to last. He had been hoping Lance would just fade away. But why would Lance fade away from a million dollar business? Lance was here to stay, and he couldn't start goofing off like his dad, Junior. At least not right away.

17

That would come later, after boredom and complacency had set in. And the realization that it didn't matter what you did; everyone had to eat and Galaxy Foods had a hot location. You'd have to work hard not to make money.

"I've been checking things out down at the warehouse," said Lance importantly. "You gotta keep an eye on those guys," he added, apparently referring to the Galaxy Foods wholesaler, United Independent Grocers, known around the store as UIG. "I let our merchandiser and the ad people and so forth know I was on board and that I'm really committed to doing a terrific job here, and that I'm real serious about the pursuit of excellence."

Lance looked pensive, and transferred his gaze from his shoe to the ceiling. "You know, Ted, sometimes people think that when you're part of a family-owned business, you're not as on top of things as some self-made guy."

"Yeah," said Ted. "People do think that sometimes."

"No one says anything. I just sense it."

"I guess you're a pretty intuitive guy, Lance."

"Yeah. Well, it's really unfair. I've got to prove myself, you know? In a way, I envy you, starting out being just some Joe Blow off the street, working your way up from box boy and all that."

"Mmm," said Ted, noting with satisfaction that Lance's ugly red pimple was still in evidence. "You sitting in on the ad meeting?"

"Yeah. I have some ideas on a new look and feel for our ad. I've already expressed it to the ad department down at UIG. In fact, I helped them put together a special layout for our grand reopening and remodeling sale, and I've asked the creative director to come up from UIG and explain it to everyone, 'cause I think we'll be using it on a weekly basis."

Ted's heart sank. "But we just did a redesign on our front page. You don't mean you've changed it again?"

"You'll see," said Lance with a twinkle, as if promising a treat to a child. "I bet you'll like it."

"That last redesign cost thousands of dollars," said Ted. "And we got a nice easy-to-read ad, real flexible so we could change the number of banner features and stuff. It took forever to fine-tune it."

"Yeah, well that layout is history," said Lance curtly as Junior and Karl came in.

"Are we having a meeting?" said Junior vaguely.

"Weekly ad meeting," said Ted. He refrained from adding that they'd met every Monday at two to go over the weekly newspaper ad for several years now.

"Our remodeling sale ad," said Karl. "I think I'll sit in. You guys might want my help. We got to be right on price for the sale."

"Good idea," said Ted reflexively, even though he hated it when Karl participated in ad meetings. The old boy dragged things on forever arguing about price points.

Then Ted chided himself for saying "good idea" automatically like that. He did a good job. He didn't have to kiss up to the Krogstads. Ted realized Lance had rattled him.

Just then, the UIG merchandiser, Lou Wells, the man who chose and priced the sale items, arrived. Lou was an eager young man who worked hard for the Krogstads, and, Ted felt, seldom got any credit for his efforts.

With Lou was another man, clearly from the UIG advertising department, the only department that allowed its employees to look the slightest bit different. Fortyish, with a shock of blond hair, he was introduced as Mel and he wore faded jeans, a hot-pink shirt, a Southwestern bolo tie, and cowboy boots with silver toes.

Lance immediately took charge of the meeting. "Mel and I worked up a new layout," he said. "It's a little more up to date, a little more exciting, more in tune with what's happening today. Why don't you explain it to the team, Mel?"

19

Mel busied himself with an easel and set a folder of black cardboard on it. "Before I show it to you," he said, "let's talk concept—let me tell you the creative rationale behind the concept."

Ted tried not to smirk. It was clear Mel still had plenty to learn about grocers. Grocers were a bunch of literal-minded can stackers. They had to be, to make a profit on tiny margins. They didn't want to hear about concepts. If Lance had hooked himself up with this guy, he was already in trouble. Ted settled back with pleasant anticipation.

"As you know," began Mel, "you share the inside pages with other independently owned and operated Galaxy Food stores. But the front and back pages are flex pages and that's where we personalize it and make you special."

"Yeah, yeah," said Karl Krogstad impatiently. "So we hit the remodeling sale hard, right?"

Lou Wells broke in with a strained voice. "Mel and Lance here put this idea together, and I'm anxious to get your reaction."

Ted looked over at Lou. He'd done a nice job of thoroughly disassociating himself from the ad. It must be pretty horrible.

"Listen," began Mel, "when you think Galaxy Foods, what comes to mind?"

"Price. Quality. Service," said Junior, who generally made an early contribution or two to every meeting before turning his furtive attention to his gold Rolex. Ted figured he'd lifted the idea from one of the banners that hung in the center aisle.

Mel waved his hand impatiently. "But all grocers say that. I mean, it's become basically, totally meaningless."

"Not to my customers it hasn't basically, totally," snapped Karl.

"Okay, okay. What I mean is, think about the name. Galaxy. What does it conjure up?" Mel spoke in the slightly patronizing tone of an elementary school teacher attempting to foster class discussion.

"Galaxy Foods," said Karl. "That's the name of the damned store. Jeez."

"Well, when Lance and I started brainstorming," said Mel with a wild gleam in his eye, "we came up with the Jetsons."

"Who the hell are they?" said Karl Krogstad. "They don't own any stores in this market."

"That cartoon show, Dad," said Junior triumphantly. He started to sing the theme song. *"Meet George Jetson . . ."* he began in a light baritone. "I used to watch it in college."

Lance coughed nervously. "It was like the Flintstones, Grandpa. But in the future."

"The Flintstones were cavemen," explained Ted solemnly.

"We're talking a kind of a sixties futuristic thing, you know," said Mel. "All streamlining and robots and stuff. Get it?"

It was apparent that Karl Krogstad didn't. "Let's see the goddamn ad," he snarled.

"Show us the ad, Mel," said Lou Wells. It was clear to Ted from his firm tone that what he really meant was "Show us the ad Mel and shut up."

"Okay," said Mel a little petulantly. He flipped open the black cardboard folder. The layout was neatly mounted and to scale. It depicted an outer space scene peppered with cartoonish white planets on a black background. Some had rings around them like Saturn. Others had craters or bands. They were all different sizes and white lines streaking off of them seemed to be meant to show they were hurtling through space. Each heavenly body had an item and price in its center, but because they were all shooting off in different directions, the type was set at odd angles on each planet.

White block letters at the top said A GALAXY OF RED HOT

DEALS and a starburst said GRAND REOPENING AND REMODEL-
ING SALE.

"Voilà" said Mel.

Junior, Karl, and Ted all twisted their heads around to
read the prices.

"Jesus Christ," said Karl Krogstad. "You're killing me.
Look at that!"

"I see what you mean, Grandpa," said Lance. "I'm disappointed, Mel. It isn't at all what I had in mind, look-wise."
It was clear to Ted that Lance had noticed the wheels were
falling off his train.

"Never mind that," said Karl. "See that dog chow price?
If we're not right on dog chow, we're dog meat. And it's the
ten-pound bag, too."

"We'll knock it down fifty cents," said Lou hastily.

"I guess you better," said Karl. "Goddamn it, Lou, we
need hot prices. The store's been torn up and our totals are
slipping bad. Plus I got to close for a week while they glue
down the linoleum so the customers don't pass out from
the fumes, and so the damned union electricians can
rewire. Meanwhile, all the inventory's just sitting there not
doing shit for me. So we gotta get them back in. Dog chow
at ten ninety-nine, that just ain't gonna cut it."

"We'll knock it down a dollar," said Lou. "No problem.
I got a special purchase on it. There's still some squoosh in
there."

"Fix it," snapped Krogstad.

"And we've got to get those prices straight up and down
and readable," said Lou.

"That's all I need," said Karl, getting red in the face.
"Mrs. Housewife throwing out her back trying to read the
damn ad."

"But setting the type at angles like that makes the ad
more dynamic, gives it movement," said Mel wriggling in
his chair. "And it engages the reader. Twisting and turning
your head means the prospect gets more involved in the

advertising communication. Your message becomes more important."

"You told me the prices would be set vertically, Mel," said Lance sternly.

"You said you liked it this way," said Mel, the sting of betrayal reducing his voice to a whine.

Karl Krogstad ignored him. "And look at that!" He pointed accusingly. "House brand cornflakes, two bucks a box. Big deal. I want some terrific price points."

"You always say you want to avoid loss leaders," said Lou.

"Of course I do. I gotta make money. I'm not in business for my health. But can't you get us a deal on those cornflakes? I don't even want them on the ad if we can't get them at one eighty-nine. Have you seen those off-brand cornflakes? They aren't even orange. Just kind of beige."

"I'll see what I can do," said Lou, jotting down a line in a small spiral-bound notebook.

"A loss leader has to be a product everybody wants," said Karl. "Not that crap."

"You know," said Ted evenly, "I'm concerned about that black background. It looks okay in the layout, I guess." He allowed a note of doubt to creep into his tone, "but when the newspaper prints it up it'll probably look all gray." He gave Lance a concerned look he hoped didn't appear patently phony. "I don't mean to be critical, Lance. I know you worked hard on this idea of yours. But I can just see it in a sick, washed-out gray."

Ted glanced over at Karl to see if he'd scored one against Lance with the old man, but Karl was, judging from the fact his head was sideways, still preoccupied with prices. "Where's the two-liter Coke you told me about?" he asked sharply.

"We're still working that deal," said Lou. "Coke or Pepsi, whatever I can get, you'll have it."

"Forget these items," said Mel. "I mean we can sort that out later, right? Let's talk about our feelings about the ad

23

itself. Lance was thinking this could be a permanent format."

"Hold the phone, Mel," said Lance. "I never . . ."

"What do you mean forget the prices? That's what this business is about and don't you forget it," said Karl. Suddenly, his eyes narrowed. "What about the grand reopening events? We got a drawing and prizes and stuff."

"Well," said Mel, "I thought they could go on the back page. I mean a trash compacter, is that a front page prize?"

Karl snorted. "I could use that trash compacter. For some of your brilliant ideas."

Mel ignored the blatant insult, and just blinked.

"Well, we got some kind of giveaway, don't we?" said Karl. "Junior, you told me you got that together."

"Seahawk key chains," said Junior. "The Hawks are doing better this season."

"Let's be frank," said Mel. "Do you really think anyone would cross the street for a Seattle Seahawks key chain?"

"Well, we've got free coffee too," said Karl Krogstad. "Absolutely free. And a personal appearance by—say!" he exclaimed, "why isn't Ginger on the front page? Ginger Jessup," shouted Karl. "The Galaxy Foods girl. She'll be here. In person."

"Oh. Right. Ginger," said Mel. "Well, do you think anyone would cross the street for a cup of coffee from Ginger Jessup?" he said. Then he answered his own question. "Maybe if she gave them a cup of coffee and a blow job," he said with a leer.

There was a deadly silence, and all eyes turned to Karl Krogstad. Everyone knew he was crazy about Ginger Jessup. In fact, while the wives of other Galaxy Foods owners had conducted a subtle campaign to get the pitchwoman canned on the grounds she looked like a cheap tart, Karl Krogstad had told UIG he'd get himself another wholesaler if Ginger ever left.

"*What* did you say about Ginger?" said Karl.

24

Mel waved his hand impatiently. "I know. Maybe we could put her in a sort of gold lamé jumpsuit thing for the personal appearance. Very Jane Jetson. Something that shows off those great bazongas."

Karl Krogstad rose slowly from his chair and stepped forward toward Mel. "You bastard," he said. "No one talks that way about Ginger. You hear me?" He grabbed the ends of Mel's bolo tie and began sliding the hunk of turquoise north.

Ted rose and put an arm on Karl's elbow. "Take it easy," he said.

Karl, his face red, backed off. "Miss Jessup and I are engaged to be married," he said. "We weren't planning to announce it just yet, but we plan to marry soon after this remodel is behind me. Don't you ever say one more word about her, or I'll twist your head off."

Then he looked at everyone else in the room, as if to spread the threat around.

4

◆

Karen Hamilton came into the living room wearing a lilac-colored chiffon dress and beamed at her two children sitting on the sofa. The fact that they were both looking sulky did nothing to dampen her motherly pride. Now that they were grown and moved out, it was so delightful to see them sitting side by side in the living room like this.

Louise, she observed, looked very pretty in black silk pants and a rose-colored silk top, cut like a T-shirt. Her heavy dark blond hair was pinned up with some wisps hanging down, and she wore lipstick for a change. Harry was wearing a gray suit.

"Stan's almost ready," she said. "You both look so nice."

"Do we have to go?" said Harry. "One of us should be at the store."

"It means a lot to Grandpa," said Karen, sitting down and arranging lilac folds around her knees.

"Don't you think it's a little corny, having an engagement party? I mean, the man's in his sixties," said Louise.

"Yeah, but she's thirty years younger," snorted Harry.

Karen sighed. "Let's try and be gracious," she said. "I feel kind of sorry for Ginger. It can't be easy for her. Everyone thinks she's just after his money."

"Gee," said Louise, sarcastically. "I wonder how they got that idea?"

"Well it isn't that easy for me, either," said Karen firmly. "My mother's only been dead a year and a half and my father takes up with that—" she stopped herself. "There's no accounting for people's tastes when it comes to getting married."

It was an awkward moment for her own husband Stan Hamilton to come into the room. Neither Louise nor Harry were fond of their stepfather. Karen had been widowed for five years when she'd married Stan several years before. A Realtor, he had come to the store asking for contributions to the Lions Club scholarship fund.

Louise and Harry were in their twenties, but when Stan came into the room they eyed him with the wariness of children.

"Hi, kids," said Stan breezily, adjusting his cuffs. He wore a rather loud sports coat and gray slacks. "All ready?"

"As ready as we'll ever be," said Harry.

"Maybe you'd feel better if you started calling her Grandma right away," said Louise with a snide smile.

"Not a bad idea," said Stan. "I think we should let the little gold digger know we're on to her."

"Stan," said Karen with forbearance, "there's nothing we can do about this. Or should, for that matter. I've just asked the children to be gracious."

"Gracious? It's their inheritance. You want them working for that harlot when your dad passes away?"

"Stan! Please!" said Karen.

"Well, face it. He's got a bad heart. If she gets the store—"

"That's right, Mom," said Harry. "She doesn't know anything about the grocery business. What if she gets everything?"

"Dad has never told me about his will and I've never asked," said Karen.

"Well, you should," said Stan. "Right, kids? I mean I'd like to help your mother here make a go of running the place someday—and make sure you kids get what's coming to you, too."

"I don't see why you expect Junior to step aside," said Karen. "He's already running things."

"The only reason Grandpa let Uncle Junior take over was because Dad died," said Harry. "And now, that little weasel Lance—"

Karen held up her hands. "Can't we all just go and have a pleasant evening? After all, we're Grandpa's guests. Everything will work out nicely. It always does in the end."

Louise looked over at her mother fondly. Mom always thought everything would turn out nicely—and it would if everyone behaved as nicely as she did. "I'm sorry, Mom," said Louise. "We must seem horrible." She turned to her brother and stepfather. "It seems to me that if we don't like the way the store is run, we should just get out and do something else."

"But it hurts me to see your mother having so little say in things," said Stan. "And I should have some rights as her husband. If I could just be more involved I'd make sure she gets a fair shake. I know a lot of my people skills could do wonders for that store of yours." The two children exchanged skeptical glances.

"I don't need anything," said Karen. She looked over at

her son. "Harry is the one who loves the grocery business. I've always hoped Dad would make a place for him."

◆

A few miles away, outside a similar suburban house, Junior Krogstad and his wife, Ellen, were getting into their Buick Riviera. Ellen, a rather plump blonde with heavy, athletic legs, struggled to keep the hem of her black dress down as she got into the car, then settled back and stroked her short mink jacket thoughtfully.

"I can't believe your dad is going to do it," she said.

"Yeah, yeah," said Junior as he yanked the car into reverse. "You've said that about a million times. Believe me, I'm not happy about it either, and neither is Lance. Just when the boy gets his break in the business, it looks like he might end up working for a young widow in a couple of years. Why can't Dad just screw her? That's what I want to know."

"That's just what I'd expect you to say," she said. "Maybe your father isn't as enthusiastic about cheap affairs and sordid one night stands as you are."

"Ease up, will you, Ellen? I told you. It's all behind me."

Ellen gave a short, bitter laugh. "It's funny, for a while I thought Ginger Jessup was one of your little playmates," she said. "Charlotte at Weight Watchers said she saw her come out of the store late one night after closing time— before you went twenty-four hours. I wondered if you weren't having her on that horible plaid sofa in the office."

"God, Ellen, you want to give it a break?" said Junior. His voice cracked. "I never touched her. I swear to God."

His wife gave him a sharp look. "I can always smell fear on you," she said, then allowed a grim little smile to pass over her features.

"Please, Ellen," he said, "don't do anything stupid tonight."

30

5

Ted wasn't looking forward to the party. For one thing, he figured he put in long days at Krogstad's Galaxy Foods. He didn't mind that, but after a week of working around the Krogstads, and making sure the store functioned properly despite them, he wasn't too keen about socializing with them on his day off.

For another thing, he knew the food would be catered from the store's deli department. Karl was simply too cheap for anything else. Ted, who'd grown up on good food, was less than enthusiastic about the greasy barbecued chicken and the pea and shrimp salad awash in mayo he knew he could expect.

31

Third, he felt the party might fall flat. No one seemed very enthusiastic about Karl Krogstad's pending nuptials besides Karl himself. (And presumably the bride-to-be, but Ted wouldn't bet money on that, either.)

Lance had gone pale when the old man had made his announcement, but managed a hearty handshake and a croaked "Congratulations, Grandpa." Junior had been silent until his father left the room, after which he'd pounded the desk and demanded "Why doesn't he just fuck her?"

It could make for a tense celebration, and Ted always felt uncomfortable when a party fell flat. It was almost a guilty feeling, as if any enterprise in which he was involved was his responsibility.

As he shaved and selected a tie—a festive red-and-navy striped silk instead of the usual uniform polyester black tie he wore at work with his apron—he told himself to forget it. All he had to do was show up, smile, have a drink, and check out the Krogstads. It might be kind of interesting to see how they were holding up.

He parted and combed his dark hair meticulously, ran a finger over his jaw and found it sufficiently smooth, checked himself out in the mirror, decided he looked good all dressed up for a change in his dark suit, and then went into the small kitchen and made himself a roast beef sandwich with thinly sliced Roma tomatoes and plenty of horseradish.

He didn't want hunger to strike while he was faced with those chicken wings from the deli. Which reminded him to bring up the fact that at the store those chicken wings seemed to sit there under the heat lamp for hours. There was no excuse for that, he thought with a frown, as he ate his sandwich. That whole deli department needed checking into. He made a note to investigate their procedures next week. He'd just read a frightening article in *Supermarket*

News about a nasty salmonella incident somewhere in the Midwest.

The party was being held in the banquet room of a mediocre Chinese restaurant in the strip mall where Krogstad's Galaxy Foods was located. Karl Krogstad owned the mall, and got a percentage of the restaurant's gross, so he was getting some of his own money back. And, because he was the landlord, he also had the clout to insist on bringing his own food and letting the restaurant just supply its watery drinks.

Ted felt a little strange handing his car keys over to Jason, who, along with some of the other box boys had been pressed into service running valet parking in front of the Happy Moon Temple Gardens.

"A lot of people show up?" he asked.

"Yeah," said Jason, pulling self-consciously at the rented white jacket that strained across his powerful torso. "And guess what? I parked her car." Jason's eyes grew round and goggly.

"What do you mean *her* car?"

"Ginger Jessup's. I recognized her from TV. Gosh, she's so beautiful. Littler than you'd think, but real pretty. And real nice. She was wearing this dress with spots on it and it was all hiked up when she got out of the car, and I couldn't help but look. She's got really great legs, you know?"

"Yeah, I suppose she does." Ted remembered seeing them when Ginger wore a bathing suit in the Galaxy Hawaiian days promotion TV spot.

"Anyway, I guess she saw me checking her out. It was like, real embarrassing," Jason blushed happily at the memory, "and she just laughed and said 'I bet you got great thighs too.' Can you believe it?"

"I'm afraid I can," said Ted. "Listen, she's old enough to be your mother, Jason."

"It was like she was coming on to me. A real movie star.

Well almost. I mean a TV star." Jason looked confused. "I think I'm in love," he said.

Ted rolled his eyes. "Settle down, will you?" he said. "You better get used to her. She'll probably spend a lot of time around the store from now on."

"Wow," said Jason. "She will?"

What the kid needed, Ted thought, was a girlfriend his own age. Or a long, cold shower. And where did that bimbella get off getting the poor kid all confused, anyway? He had a sinking feeling that Ginger Jessup was going to be trouble. It had already started, right here at the curb.

Inside, the banquet room with its red-flocked wallpaper was garishly lit with tasseled Chinese lamps. Before Ted had a chance to get himself a drink, he was chagrined to find himself cornered by Leonard LeBlanc, the seafood manager. Leonard had probably been lurking at the door in hopes of hooking anyone who came in. Fishing imagery came easily when you were thinking of Leonard. Seafood was his life.

"Hi Ted," he said cheerily. "How are you?"

"Just fine," said Ted. "How are things?"

He regretted this last remark instantly. "Well," Leonard said, "seafood-wise, things are looking up. Salmon prices have stabilized but they're still good. Farmed product has brought some real consistency to supply. Of course, it doesn't have the texture of wild product, but now salmon is a year-round commodity. We've been doing real well with it since we put it on ad."

"Fine, fine," said Ted. "Glad to hear it."

"Cod's not looking so good, though," said Leonard, his face darkening. "Quotas have been slashed in the North Atlantic, and the price of Pacific cod is slowly inching upwards. I'm looking at some alternative species. Alaskan pollock is still a good buy, but there's still name confusion. Some people think it's Atlantic pollock, which of course is another species entirely."

"Is that right?" said Ted.

"I'm doing what I can to educate the consumer," said Leonard as Ted inched away. "I'm looking at New Zealand hoki and tilapia, too. And Nile perch."

"I think I'll go perch over by the bar," said Ted.

"Hey, I guess I could go on forever," said Leonard. "But I sometimes think the rest of you guys don't really understand seafood."

"That's why we've got you," said Ted, slapping him on the shoulder, and striding purposefully away. God, he thought to himself. The way Leonard talks, you'd think we actually made a buck on the seafood department. Maybe he'll quiet down when we get him that new lobster tank. Ted had heard that they took a lot of daily maintenance.

He moseyed past a table with food, just out of curiosity. There were the chicken wings and the pea and shrimp salad, as well as the perennial cheese ball crusted with crushed walnuts and some vegetable platters. He noticed Marvella, the deli manager, standing nearby. An ample woman, swathed now in purple with a lot of rhinestones, she looked down at the table with such pride, Ted took pity on her and made a big deal of swirling some cauliflower in dip. "Looks good," he said with a smile.

Up at the bar, he jettisoned the cauliflower and got himself a vodka tonic. Normally, Ted drank wine, but he figured vodka was a generic product and the wine here would be lousy. He nodded at Junior, who was hunkered down over a bourbon in businesslike fashion.

A little to one side stood Karl Krogstad, holding hands with a beaming Ginger Jessup. "Come over here, Ted," said the old man with a wide grin. "Meet the little lady."

Ted went over and shook her hand solemnly.

Ginger was wearing a black-and-white polka-dot dress that showed a lot of old-fashioned–looking cleavage on top and a lot of shapely leg below. Her orange hair and her makeup were shiny, and her eyes were narrowed—pushed

35

into slits by a giant smile, and round peach-colored cheeks.

She gave him a murmur of greeting, pressed his hand in her small one, and gave off a musky cloud of perfume before she turned to greet another arrival.

He backed away toward the bar. Ted had always thought she looked silly in her TV spots. But seeing her in the flesh, he found himself bowled over. His first thought was that there was no justice in the world when an old bastard like Karl Krogstad could snag himself a babe like this. She had a cartoonish quality, it was true, but there was more to her than that. Her face looked sweet and yielding, and her breasts, propped up into beautiful mounds of soft flesh—

Ted's reverie was broken by a snide female voice at his side. "They aren't real, you know."

He yanked his eyes away from Ginger's magnificent chest, and turned to face Louise McDonald. A Krogstad on her mother's side, tall and lanky, she seemed strangely angular and rangy next to Ginger Jessup.

"Okay," said Ted, "I guess you caught me staring."

"You and every other guy in the place." Louise leaned on the bar and ordered a white wine. She was always slouching. "The testosterone level around here would probably pin the meter in the red zone," she said sharply.

Ted was startled. Louise, who ran the video department, and seemed to spend most of her day watching videos of old black-and-white movies on a tiny monitor behind her counter, had always struck him as a shy, quiet young woman.

"When a woman wears a dress like that, guys are going to check it out," said Ted, trying to muster some dignity. "Sorry, but that's just the way it is." Louise had made him feel like a real jerk. "I wasn't drooling or anything." This was a flat-out lie, but Ted believed it as he said it. He touched the knot of his tie and smoothed down his hair, nervous little grooming gestures that seemed to restore his sense of self-respect.

36

"I'm sorry," said Louise, in a softer voice. "I guess I sound like a real bitch. It's just hard to get used to having her in the family." Her blue-gray eyes got big and sad and fixed themselves on Ted. "You look different without your apron," she said.

"You look different without yours," said Ted, who felt an urge to run his eyes down the long length of her—she was wearing slinky black pants and a pink top. He resisted, however, because he'd just barely managed to dissuade her from thinking he was a total sleaze. No doubt about it, that Ginger Jessup was trouble. Instead, he smiled nicely, hoping it didn't come across as a leer.

Louise shifted herself around until she was leaning backwards on the bar. "I guess you've been working with my cousin Lance lately."

Ted shrugged. "Sort of. I'm supposed to show him the ropes. But he hasn't been around much lately."

"I noticed." She sipped her wine. "Any idea what he's going to be doing on a more permanent basis?" Her tone sounded deceptively casual.

"You mean after I teach him everything I know?"

"Yeah."

"No. That's up to your uncle and your grandfather, I guess." Ted was surprised Louise didn't know. This could be a good sign. Maybe they weren't planning to bust Ted back to box boy just yet, anyway.

Louise twisted a strand of dark blond hair around one long finger. "Harry has a lot to contribute," she said. "Harry really loves this business."

"Your brother is a real good worker," said Ted. He'd wondered why Lance was being groomed for big things, and his cousin Harry, Karl's other grandson, spent his days feeding boxes into the crusher and stocking shelves.

"That's what he says about you," said Louise. She turned and smiled at him.

"That's gratifying," said Ted, noting the irony that the

37

Krogstad who appreciated his efforts was the one farthest from the center of power.

"It's true. You're always running all over the store. You never even stop and chat with me. There I am trapped behind that video counter all day." She gave him a cool, steady smolder, like something from one of the old movies she watched all day.

Ted knew from experience that he tended to be dense where women were concerned, but an idea was slowly dawning in his mind. He leaned toward Louise with a serious look.

"Can I ask you a question?" he said.

She looked pleased. "Sure."

"How come when we talk, you always slouch? Is it my imagination, or do you always slouch when we talk?"

She bit her lip a little nervously. "I think it's because I'm taller than you are," she said.

He nodded. Ted had learned that when tall women slouched around him, it was usually a good sign. "I see. Well, you look uncomfortable slouching. Why don't you just stand up straight? I don't find it particularly threatening that you're taller than I am. If you even are."

"I'm five-nine," said Louise. "How tall are you?"

"I'm five-nine too," said Ted. He was lying by half an inch. "So we're the same size. Stand up straight and I'll show you."

She put down her drink and straightened up. Her shoulders broadened, her breasts emerged from the curve of her stance, her hips evened out. Ted watched her fall into alignment, then stepped forward just a little closer in the natural conversational zone. "See. We're the same size," he said, pinning her big blue-gray eyes with his brown ones. He figured if their eyes locked, she'd figure they were the same size.

Wait a minute, he said to himself. You can't flirt with her. As usual, disaster compressed itself in his mind. He imag-

38

ined their first kiss, maybe out on the loading dock, their hearts beating wildly beneath their aprons. He imagined a passionate affair, followed by a passionate breakup. He imagined tears, the tense exchange of personal property from each other's apartments, broken hearts. And if things got messy, who would have to leave Krogstad's Galaxy Foods? A Krogstad on her mother's side or the hired help?

Ted stepped back a pace, just as they heard the scream.

They turned to see Ginger Jessup's face streaked with tears. Karl Krogstad, red in the face, was mopping off her dress. Junior Krogstad's wife Ellen was facing her, and in her limp hand was an empty drink glass. Ellen looked defiant and pleased with herself.

"Oh, no," said Louise.

Ted found himself hustling over to the scene. It was second nature to him to react to a spill, he supposed. A second later, Junior came over and put a restraining arm around Ellen. "What did you do?" he said.

Ginger was sniffling now, and turned her face to Karl Krogstad's shoulder. "Get your wife out of here now," hissed the old man. "I'll talk to you later."

Lance came up and stood next to his parents. "Gosh," he said, "what's going on?"

Ginger sobbed again. There was an ice cube nestling in her cleavage. Junior leaned over as if to remove it, but seemed to think better of it. Karl followed his eyes, and plucked it away himself.

"Lance, get your mother out of here," said Karl Krogstad. "We don't want a scene."

Other people were coming over to the corner, and Ted stood between Ginger and the curious. "No big deal," he said, holding up his hands to obscure the view of the weeping woman. "Just a little spill. Miss Jessup is going to have to clean her dress." He gestured for Karl to lead her away.

Karl picked up Ted's cue. "A spilled drink and some bride's jitters, folks," he said amiably. Ted cleared a path

39

and the couple followed him out of the room. Ginger's head was up now, and she smiled through her tears, but a sooty trail of mascara worked its way down her cheeks.

Karen Hamilton rushed to her side. "Is everything okay?" she said solicitously to Ginger.

"It's not true," said Ginger. "It's not."

"Of course it isn't" said Karl."

"Did you come in separate cars?" said Ted to Karl. "Yeah."

"Jason, get Miss Jessup's car." Ted gave him a look that said "Do it now and don't react."

"I'll drive her home," said Karen. "If she wants."

"No," said Karl. "I will."

"But Dad," said Karen, "it's your party. If you leave, people will talk."

"Okay. Okay." said Karl.

"I'll tell them something," said Ted. "These things happen." He wondered what he meant. What had actually happened wasn't too clear, but it appeared Ellen Krogstad had thrown a drink on her future stepmother-in-law.

Before Jason returned with Ginger's car, however, the group gathered on the curb was treated to the spectacle of Junior and Ellen driving by in their Buick. Junior's voice came clearly through as they cruised by. "That was a really stupid thing to do."

"Oh dear," said Karen gently.

Lance appeared on the sidewalk, smoothing back his hair. "Gosh Ginger, I can't imagine what happened. Mom sometimes kind of loses it. I'm sure we can talk it all out. Get everything out in the open." He glanced back and forth between Ginger and his grandfather. For just an instant, Ted thought he saw a flicker of satisfaction in Lance's face. "I'm sure we can talk it all out."

Ginger seemed to catch it too. "There's plenty we can talk about," she said in a hard, cold voice. She sniffed, rubbed her mascara off her cheeks and stood up straight.

"I'm going back in there," she said, with a toss of her head.

"Listen, all of you," said Karl Krogstad in a voice deep with emotion. "If anyone ever makes Ginger unhappy again, they're out. Got that. O-U-T."

6

It wasn't until he went back to work that Ted heard exactly what had happened. Jerry, one of the butchers, told him. Jerry was making kabobs, and Ted stood back from the splattering blood as the cleaver hit the chopping block with rhythmic precision. "From what I hear, I missed the makings of a really good cat fight," said Jerry with a thwack of his cleaver. "Old Ellen just went up to Ginger and told her she thought she had a lot of nerve marrying the old man when she'd been screwing his son. And then the bitch threw a drink in the bimbo's face." He laughed heartily. Jerry was a union guy and didn't care if he gossiped about the Krogstads to management.

43

Marvella in Deli had more information. Her technique was to fake concern for the family. "I guess the older Mr. Krogstad doesn't believe what Ellen said," she confided as she tossed celery and imitation crab into her Neptune salad. "But he's still terribly upset. It really is a sad thing for the whole family. Such a shame." She tossed a knife into her stainless-steel sink with a clatter.

Out of respect for the Krogstads, Ted kept his distance while things simmered down. Although he always smiled at Louise as he walked by, and brief fantasies of their imaginary embrace on the loading dock raced through his mind, he told himself he should probably keep his distance from her whatever happened.

Karl didn't show up for a few days, and neither did Junior, or, mercifully, Lance. Ted took the opportunity to finalize details for the grand reopening. The proper produce awnings were in place, the sale items approved, the ad looked good. Leonard LeBlanc got his lobster tank, and Ted nursed him through the crisis when the first batch of lobsters dropped dead. After a temperature adjustment, their replacements seemed to be thriving.

Three days later, Junior, looking worn and drawn, showed up. "Step into my office, Ted, will you?"

"Things have been a little tense lately," he said. "I guess you know there was a scene at Dad's party."

"These things happen," said Ted.

"Yeah. Well, my wife isn't herself lately. She's had a lot of trouble with the, er, change of life."

Ted nodded understandingly.

"Anyway, we're sending her to a clinic for a while."

Good move, thought Ted to himself. Plead insanity. It's your only chance.

"Rest, relaxation. Down in Palm Springs."

"I hope she'll be feeling better soon," said Ted.

"Yeah. Well, my dad may have gotten the wrong impression," said Junior. "By the way," he said with a look of fear in his eye, "has he been in?"

"Uh, no," said Ted. "But I expect him soon. He wouldn't miss the grand reopening."

"Yeah. How many days we got?" said Junior vaguely. Ted wondered if he'd been on a bender since the party and lost track of time. Presumably he'd been sufficiently sober to pack his wife into the happy home.

"The store closes down for a week starting Monday," said Ted. "The linoleum guys and the electricians will be here."

"Good, good," said Junior vaguely. "How's everything looking?"

"Just fine," said Ted.

"We get those key chains?" said Junior, his mind fastening on the one small detail he'd contributed to the festivities.

"Yeah." Ted imagined the staff sweeping a gross of them out of the store after the big sale. "And we got some more prizes for the drawing. A microwave and a VCR. We got them in time to put them in the ad."

"Fine, fine," said Junior. "I'm sorry Lance won't be here to help."

"That's too bad," said Ted. "But we'll manage."

"He's gone skiing. Poor kid. He was so worried about his mother."

"I can understand that," said Ted, trying to sound sympathetic.

The phone rang, and Junior picked it up. "Oh, hi Dad," he said, his voice cracking with fear. "I've got a lot to tell you. Ellen is, poor Ellen, you see—"

Ted didn't know whether to leave or not. He figured he'd wait until he was dismissed. He wanted to find out what he could.

"What's that? No. I don't know. Let me check with Ted. Oh, okay."

Junior handed the phone to Ted. "It's Dad" he said.

"Hello," said Ted, trying to sound as if everything were normal.

"Have you heard from Ginger?" said Karl Krogstad in a desperate voice. "Has she called the store?"

"No. Not that I know of. I'll check." Ted ruffled through some pink phone messages with one hand. "Sorry, she hasn't."

"Okay," said Karl Krogstad. "I'll leave another message on her machine. Call me at home if you hear from her. It's urgent."

"Got it," said Ted.

"Anyway, we'll see her at the grand reopening," said Karl. "She's a real pro. She'll be there." The old man sounded plaintive.

"Hope everything's all right," said Ted. "Is she missing?"

"Of course not," said the old man in his usual irritable tone. "We've just crossed communication. Call me if you hear from her."

"Let me tell him about Ellen," whispered Junior urgently.

Ted imagined Junior was eager to present his insanity defense. The berserk irrational wife was definitely the only way to play it. Lance had apparently decided discretion was the better part of valor and had simply left town. Not a bad move either, thought Ted. Before Junior could get on the line, however, the old man hung up. He left Junior in the office gnawing at his cuticles.

Ted felt restive while the store was closed. He came in and checked on the linoleum guys a few times and when they were through, and the electricians had finished too, and the shelves were all set, he came in and did a walk-through. The store looked nice. He ran into Harry McDonald, Louise's brother, doing the same thing. They both agreed the remodeling was a real success.

"We should really blow some product out of here," said

46

Harry approvingly as they passed an end-aisle bin of house brand cornflakes, a dollar eighty-nine. "The pricing looks good." Harry, who normally had a sullen look on his face, seemed quite excited about the store's new look.

"Now that we're open twenty-four hours, it's never quiet like this. Just all that terrific-looking product sitting on the shelves." He sighed happily, then looked concerned. "But I miss the customers. The place feels kind of eerie like this, doesn't it?"

Just then the two men heard a sound over in seafood and hustled over there. Leonard LeBlanc was bent over his lobster tank, crooning to his crustaceans.

"Just checking up on my babies," said Leonard. "You know, there's a lot of interest in lobster on the West Coast, even though most people here grew up on crab. It'll be interesting to see how we do. I'd like to get some live Dungeness in here next.

"Speaking of crab, we've got ourselves a real nice buy on snow crab for the opening, and I've got a big case of brown king crab, and even a big box of red crab legs in the freezer. Most of that goes to the restaurant trade, but I managed to get myself some. Eleven bucks a pound, but you know, there's always a market for real top end stuff. Of course, the glory days of king crab was back in the fifties. Now, the resource is considerably scarcer."

"Sounds great," said Ted, backing away.

When he and Harry were out of earshot, Harry said "How much do we make on seafood?"

"Hardly anything," said Ted. "Not after you account for shrink. The stuff's full of water. It's a loss leader."

"I bet we'd eliminate some of that shrink if we didn't have that open case," said Harry with a frown.

"I'll check into it," said Ted, although he tended to avoid any discussion with the seafood manager. It was too time consuming, and you tended to come away with a lecture on the price of cod blocks or the perils of freezer burn.

47

"Well," said Harry at the door, "I'll see you at the opening. Should be pretty hectic."

The morning of the remodeling opening was hectic, but exciting. Ted found himself rushing out into the lot with the box boys rounding up stray carts. Karen Hamilton handed out free carnations and Seahawks key chains at the front door, and pointed the customers to a stainless-steel coffee urn.

The aisles were agreeably clogged and every checkstand was open. The prices were hot, no doubt about it. The only missing element was Ginger Jessup. Scheduled for a ten o'clock appearance, she hadn't showed up. No customer, however, asked about her.

Karl Krogstad had been there all morning, holed up in his office. Ted was shocked that he hadn't been around to supervise the final details of the opening. This morning, however, he came into the store, glowered at everyone, and went up to the office.

He never came back down, which startled Ted. Karl had been so excited about the grand reopening, and he wasn't even down on the floor enjoying all the action. Ted went up there, and decided to step into his office and tell him how well things were going. He found the old man sitting at his desk with his head on the blotter.

"Mr. Krogstad," said Ted with concern, "are you all right?" He wondered if the old man was having a heart attack, and mentally reviewed the CPR techniques he'd learned.

"They drove her away," said Karl. "My family. They drove her away with lies. She's gone."

"We'll find her," said Ted, wondering if they would. He was so upset to see Karl Krogstad falling apart like this, he was ready to promise him anything. "Come on, come over to the window and take a look. The store is jammed. We're doing gangbusters down there. We keep running out of carts. I bet we total thirty grand today."

48

Karl Krogstad showed a flicker of interest and went over to the two-way mirror. "A pretty good day, huh?" he said.

"You bet," said Ted. "Look at them going for those cornflakes. You were right to get that price down. It's really moving."

There was indeed a cluster of shoppers around the end-aisle bin. But then an extraordinary thing happened. They all backed off simultaneously. From above, it looked like a flower opening. Then, even through the glass, Ted heard a woman scream.

He ran for the door and pounded down the stairs, careening into Leonard LeBlanc.

"We've got a problem in seafood," said Leonard. "Remember that case of king crab legs I told you about?"

"Not now, Len" said Ted, running over to the end of aisle eight.

When he got there, Leonard LeBlanc was still in pursuit, but Ted didn't hear him. He pushed aside two customers, one of whom was gagging, and another of whom was sobbing, and peered into the end-aisle bin. Next to him, a woman folded her little child's face into her skirt to shield its eyes.

A woman's naked arm emerged from the jumble of cereal boxes. Ted touched the pale flesh, then shouted at Leonard to call the police. Leonard just stood there staring.

"Step back everybody, please," he said. "Stay calm. There's been an accident. Leonard, call nine one one. Now."

Even though the arm was cold, Ted found himself tearing at the bin, tossing out boxes of cereal in an irrational desire to free the woman attached to the arm. The boxes hit the floor and split open, the cornflakes making a rattling sound as they skidded over the newly waxed linoleum.

"Jason," shouted Ted, "Get some product up around here." Ted found himself pushing away gawkers. Soon,

49

Jason and another courtesy clerk arrived with a hand truck of paper-towel boxes, which they used to throw up a wall around the end-aisle bin. It was standard procedure when a customer had a heart attack or an epileptic seizure.

Ted stayed inside the wall, dimly aware of the voices of the customers behind it. He continued to pull at cereal boxes and threw them on the ground behind him. Soon, a hank of hair appeared between the boxes, and then a ruddy face with glazed-over eyes and a smooth white throat. To Ted's horror, the body appeared to be naked. He stood back and stopped pulling at the boxes. There was no point in it, he saw now. At the base of the throat were two purple marks. Ted knew at once that they were the marks of two thumbs, thumbs that had choked the breath and the life out of Ginger Jessup.

7

◆

The customers had been cleared out of the store, but the barricade of paper-towel boxes remained when Seattle homicide detectives Lukowski and MacNab stood at the end of aisle three, staring into the cornflakes bin, blinking as the flash from the medical examiner's camera went off.

"Come on. You must recognize her. You've seen her on TV. The Galaxy Foods girl," said MacNab, a florid, chunky man in a loud sports coat. "Body looks real fresh, dosen't it?"

"I don't watch that much TV," said Lukowski, younger, taller, and slimmer with prematurely gray hair and a lean face. "But she looks kind of familiar."

"My wife hates her," said MacNab. "Hated her," he corrected himself. "Says she looks like a slut in those commercials. She's a celebrity. This will be a big case."

"She looks kind of pathetic now," said Lukowski, noting the red patchiness on the smooth skin, the unrealistic orange hair springing back from the dead, slack-mouthed face, the glassy green-eyed stare. Delicately, technicians removed more cornflakes boxes, exposing the body's breasts and torso.

"Nice knockers," said MacNab, managing to convey a certain reverence for the dead in his tone.

"Yeah, but they're fake," said Lukowski. "Implants." He found this a rather pitiful touch.

"You're right," said MacNab, nodding. "Working vice you get so you can spot a boob job a mile away." He shook his head sadly. "A guy could break a couple of ribs slamming into those things full tilt, you know what I mean?"

Lukowski turned away. "What the hell is she doing in the cornflakes?" he said. "This is definitely squirrelly."

Technicians removed more cereal boxes.

"I mean," continued Lukowski, "isn't this store open twenty-four hours? How'd he get her in there?"

MacNab, hands in pockets, continued to observe the scene. "Looks like she wasn't a natural redhead," he said.

Upstairs, in the office, Karl Krogstad watched the scene from the two-way mirror. His hands were in fists, and his face was red. "God!" he shouted. "Look at that! They should cover her with a sheet or something. Those bastards. They gotta have respect!" He went to the door, and Ted headed him off.

"Settle down, Mr. Krogstad," he said. "Don't upset yourself. Sit down over here." He led him to a sofa. "They're just doing their job. They said for us to wait up here."

Krogstad clutched his chest, and his face screwed up with pain.

"Hey!" said Ted. "Are you all right?"

"It's just angina," said Krogstad. "Get me my pills, will you?"

Ted rummaged in the desk drawer for Karl's pills. The old man put one under his tongue, closed his eyes, and took a deep breath.

Ted led him to the sofa and sat him down. "Want something? A glass of water or something?"

"Nope," said Karl, his voice sounding calm now. "All I want to do is find out who did this to Ginger and kill him with my bare hands."

"Try and relax," said Ted. He leaned over him with concern. "Are you sure you're all right?"

"Listen," said Krogstad fiercely, grabbing Ted's name badge and pulling him down so their faces were about three inches apart. "You're smart. I want you to help me. It's gotta be one of my goddamn relatives. They're all leeches anyway, and now one of them's done this. Stolen Ginger from me."

"We don't know what happened," said Ted, trying to sound reasonable, although the same thought had occurred to him. "Anything could have happened. It might be some horrible accident."

"Bullshit!" said the old man. "I saw those marks on her throat." His voice caught. "They didn't want me to marry Ginger and leave them out in the cold when I died. I'm not stupid, you know."

"I know you're not," said Ted, feeling extremely uncomfortable as he stared into the old man's watery blue eyes.

"And neither are you. Help me nail whoever did this," said Karl fiercely. "The cops don't need to get involved. I'll take care of it personally. What have I got to lose? Not a damn thing. I'll be lucky to live another couple of years anyway."

"Don't get so agitated," said Ted, pulling himself away and smoothing down his tie and apron.

"Find out who did this," snapped the old man. "Let's

keep the cops out of this. I never liked cops. You grab a shoplifter and call the cops, what do they do? The guy's back in the store in a week."

Ted, trying to soothe the old man and prevent another attack, decided to humor him. "Sure, Mr. Krogstad," he said. "I'll see what I can find out. I'll get right on it."

The old man leaned back and closed his eyes. "Good," he said.

Behind him, Ted heard a throat clearing. He turned around to face Lukowski and MacNab.

"We understand how upset you are," said Lukowski. "Naturally you're upset. But please, let the police handle the investigation. We do this for a living."

MacNab gave Ted a heavy-lidded look of contempt. "Yeah," he said. "Let us do our job and you do yours. We won't tell you how to bag groceries."

Ted was torn between explaining to the detectives that he had no intention of playing detective, or simply shutting up so as not to let Karl Krogstad hear he wasn't serious when he said he'd get right on it. He decided to just shut up. Looking like a jerk in front of a couple of cops was better than appearing insincere to your boss. Cops seemed to think civilians were basically jerks anyway, Ted had noticed.

"We have a couple of questions," said the taller, younger one. "Perhaps we can talk to Mr. Krogstad here in that office." He indicated a door.

"He's had a terrible shock and he's just had an angina attack," said Ted. "He's really stressed-out right now."

"It'll just take a minute or so," said Lukowski.

"The body—that is the victim—is his fiancée," explained Ted, glancing nervously over at Karl.

Lukowski raised an eyebrow and looked at Karl with new interest.

"We're very sorry, Mr. Krogstad," said the other detective. "Please accept our sympathy." He looked genuinely

54

mournful. Ted noted his vibrant glen plaid sports coat and wondered why a homicide detective would wear something that made him look like a racetrack tout. They should wear dark suits, like funeral directors.

Karl rose wearily from the sofa. "Thank you," he said simply. "If you gentlemen want to come in my office, I'll be glad to answer your questions."

Karl was so compliant and courteous, Ted really feared for his health, but he wasn't going to argue with Karl at this point.

"Mind if I go down there and check on the store?" said Ted. "We've got customers hanging around outside that police line. I'd like to tell them something."

"Okay," said MacNab. "You're the manager, right?"

"Assistant manager," said Ted.

"Okay. But stick around."

"I'm not going anywhere," said Ted, insulted at the suggestion. He couldn't imagine a bigger operational headache than a murdered woman in an end-aisle display, and he didn't trust Junior to handle things properly. Ted could foresee plenty of problems. The PR fallout was going to be horrendous. To think, just a few days ago he'd been worried about rancid mayonnaise in the deli salads.

A forced closure meant he'd have to redo all the work schedules. If they stayed closed too long, the perishables would start perishing. Seafood would be the first to go, and poor Leonard LeBlanc would be inconsolable. But produce, meat, and dairy could be affected too. Ted sighed, and went downstairs, ignoring the knot of people clustered around the end of aisle eight.

Outside the store, there was a yellow police line, and on the other side of it a bunch of customers. Some of them were waving the special coupon books. "When are you opening again?" demanded a large woman in a muumuu. "These coupons are good for one day only."

Raising his hands in a calming, vaguely papal gesture,

Ted announced in a loud voice: "We will honor these coupon books for the next seven days. We regret any inconve-
nience to our customers. Sale prices will be in effect after
we reopen."

"What the hell's going on in there," demanded an el-
derly man in a Seattle Mariners baseball cap.

"There's been a terrible accident," said Ted. Then, because he knew they'd hear it on the news anyway, and
because he seldom got to make any dramatic pronounce-
ments, Ted said "Ginger Jessup, the Galaxy Food girl, is
dead."

There was a slight gasp and the old man in the baseball
cap said "You mean the redhead with the big . . . "

"Yes," said Ted solemnly. "It's a tragic moment for all of
us at Galaxy Foods. The police are investigating her untimely death now. Please, go back to your homes, and
remember, we will honor all coupons."

"Well, what if you haven't got the item when we come
back?" said a pinched-looking woman. Ted glanced at the
coupon book she clutched and blanched when he realized
it said "Killer Prices" in big yellow letters.

"Please bear with us," said Ted. "There's been a tragic
death." He tried not to let his disapproval show. A person
had died. This customer acted as if she'd be glad to root
around in the jumble of cornflakes boxes around Ginger's
body, just to take advantage of the dollar eighty-nine price,
limit three per family. "On items that are not in stock when
you return, we will offer you a rain check," he said with
dignity. He bent his head a little as if overcome by grief,
and the crowd moved off murmuring sympathetically.

Upstairs in his office, Karl Krogstad was leaning over his
desk. "I loved her," he said. "It's that simple. She was
young and beautiful. She had a great body."

"We understand," said MacNab.

56

"You hear about a lot of older guys with young, beautiful women. People laugh. They think the old fool is being taken for a ride. But it's not like that at all."

Lukowski nodded encouragingly.

"I loved my wife, God bless her. She was a good woman, raised our two kids and still put in fifty-hour weeks at the checkstand when we were starting out.

"But this was different. I only had a few years left. And Ginger was willing to give me a couple of years of her youth." His eyes filled with tears. "My family will try and tell you she was after my dough." He snorted. "Ridiculous. Ginger had a great career of her own. Why, if she hadn't been so devoted to Galaxy Foods, she could have gone to Hollywood. With her looks and zip, she could have been a star. Like Zsa Zsa Gabor or something."

"Do you have any idea who might have wanted to harm her?" said Lukowski.

"Who would have wanted to harm a beautiful woman like that?" he said, shaking his head.

"I don't know," said Lukowski. "Were there any ex-boy-friends in the picture? Someone who might have been jealous?"

Karl shook his head. "Of course not," he said. "There was only me. I was the only man in her life. Not that she didn't have plenty of opportunities, mind you. But she always told me she'd been waiting for Mr. Right for a long time."

Lukowski and MacNab exchanged a quick, skeptical glance.

8

"What the heck are you doing, Harry?"

Ted had discovered Harry McDonald hunched over the L'eggs panty hose display, rotating plastic egg-shaped containers. This struck Ted as odd. This display was the work of the L'eggs rep, a blond young woman with short skirts and great legs who came in periodically and faced the shelves.

"Shh!" Harry whispered fiercely, straightening a row of Desert Tan queen-sized support hose. "Shoplifter."

Ted, trying to look casual, glanced out of the corner of his eye at a young man in a parka with a backpack on his back about twenty feet away, further up the aisle.

"Shall we say something?" whispered Ted.

"Hell no," hissed Harry. "I want to get him outside the store. Back off, will you. He'll rabbit."

"You call the cops," said Ted. "I'll follow him out the door."

Ted moseyed down to the aisle, away from the man in the parka, vaguely nervous at Harry's intensity. Harry, a big hulking youth, had always been a mystery to Ted. He worked diligently, but quietly, and usually with a scowl on his face.

Ted positioned himself near the front door, pretending to show interest in the bulletin board. He read an ad for a used pickup truck and a day-care center and then slowly turned around. To his annoyance, Harry wasn't up in the office calling the cops. He was after his quarry over near the bakery now, lurking behind a display of French bread like something out of a cheap spy novel. The man in the parka, looking perfectly at ease, had drifted over to the magazine rack, and now seemed to be making his way to the quick-check lane. The man grabbed a pack of gum and put it down on the counter.

The man paid for the gum and walked toward the door, and Ted prepared to follow him quietly out. He was a little reluctant to speak to him. After all, he only had Harry's word for it that the guy had been stealing. There was no better way to alienate a customer for life than to falsely accuse him. And besides, Harry hadn't called the cops. They'd have to get him back into the store and hold him.

Ted sized up the guy—something Ted, at five-eight and a half, had learned to do a long time ago. The guy was definitely taller, but then a lot of people were. It was hard to tell what kind of shape he was in under that parka, but his face looked kind of wimpy.

While Ted was mulling over just what approach to take, the man walked out the door. Before Ted had a chance to step out after him, Harry came hurtling through the door, a horrible primal yell coming out of him. The man in the parka glanced over his shoulder and took off fast. But he made the mistake of looking over his shoulder once again, and careened into a pile of Presto logs in front of the store.

A second later, Harry was all over him, and the guy was whimpering. "Stop," he yelled. "Why are you hurting me?"

"You son of a bitch. You ripped me off!" screamed Harry. Before Ted knew what was happening, Harry had the guy by the shoulders and was slamming him face down against the Presto logs.

"Wait a sec," said Ted, trying to maneuver himself in between Harry and his victim. "Just hang on."

"Jesus!" screamed the man. "I just went in for a pack of gum and now you're assaulting me."

"Let's take a look in that backpack," said Harry, all red in the face now, and huffing and puffing. He pushed Ted aside and pulled off the straps, twirling the guy around and yanking the pack off his back.

"I'm bleeding," said the man, touching his temple and examining his fingers. It was true. There was a gash on his head, frosted with sawdust from the Presto logs.

Harry didn't bother to look up. He tore into the backpack, and pulled out a notebook, a cardigan sweater, and a paperback copy of a book on stress management. He threw them on the ground one by one.

Ted took out a handkerchief and dabbed at the man's wound. "I'm sorry," he said.

"I just went in to buy some gum and your friend here went ballistic," said the man. "He assaulted me for no reason."

Harry threw the backpack down on the ground in disgust. "So where's the salsa?" he demanded, pulling back his arm as if he were about to backhand the man across the face. "I saw you take it."

"What salsa?" said the man, a trace of fear creeping into his voice as he rearranged his parka.

"What do you mean, 'what salsa,' " sneered Harry. "Old El Paso brand. The eight-ounce jar. Extra mild."

Harry certainly knew his inventory, thought Ted. "Hey!" he said to Harry. "Calm down. I'll handle this."

"He's ripping me off!" shouted Harry, yanking at the zipper on the man's parka. He tore it open and was rewarded with a jar of salsa falling to the ground and smashing. The man looked down at his feet and the reddish splat.

"What else you got?" demanded Harry, reaching into the sleeves and producing a couple of avocados and a bag of chips.

Ted started working the pockets now, ripping at Velcro and discovering refried beans, a packet of guacamole mix, a pound of ground beef, and three tomatoes.

"Well," said Ted, "I guess it was going to be fiesta night over at your house tonight, huh?"

"I bought this stuff at another store, earlier," the guy said. "I don't have to take this kind of treatment." He glanced down at the paperback book, now spattered with salsa on the pavement. "I've been under a lot of stress lately."

"You got a receipt?" said Ted. "Come on up to the office, and we'll take a look at your receipt." Ted gathered up the man's things and put them back in the backpack, gathering up the groceries too.

With a Neanderthal scowl, Harry grabbed the man, put him in a half nelson and marched him back into the store.

"Take it easy," said Ted, alarmed. "He'll go easy."

"I want to make this experience as unpleasant as possible for him," said Harry through clenched teeth as he dragged his prisoner past startled customers.

"You don't need to make a scene," said Ted. "People are watching." He grabbed a bag from checkstand three and put all the items in it.

"Then maybe they'll get the picture," said Harry firmly,

now half dragging the man up the stairs to the office "that shoplifting's a crime."

Karl Krogstad was there, going over the books. He looked up with a gleam in his eye.

"Got me a thief," said Harry, beaming happily.

Ted went over to the phone and called 911. When he turned back, he discovered Harry had the man in a full nelson now, with his arms pinned back and his head at an awkward angle. What was most disturbing, however, was that Karl Krogstad was striding up to the guy, hitching up his belt purposefully, then making his hand into a fist and swinging it backward as if he were about to gut punch him.

"Wait!" said Ted, dropping the phone and rushing over just in time to seize Karl's fist. "We can't do that. We can't just work him over. He'll sue."

Krogstad shook off Ted's arm. "Okay, okay," he said. "But I'd sure like to pop him one. If there's anything I hate, it's a goddamned thief."

"Here's the stuff he took," said Ted, hoping to distract Karl by indicating the items. "I watched him go through the checkstand and buy a pack of gum."

"I saw him lift the salsa," said Harry, puffing a little, as the guy struggled. "The Old El Paso. It's a coupon item. We lost it in the struggle."

"I don't know what came over me," said the shoplifter with a catch in his voice. "I've never done anything like this before. I've just been so stressed out lately."

"What a country," said Karl Krogstad, ignoring his whining. "A man steals from you, then when you want to hit him, which is perfectly natural, he threatens to sue."

"I didn't threaten to sue," said the man in a raspy voice. "Let's just forget the whole thing."

"Forget it?" said Karl Krogstad with a snort of contempt. "I've got half a mind to take you out behind the loading dock and smash your face. I never forget a thief." He looked up at Harry with a grim little smile. "Never. Right Harry?"

To Ted's surprise, Harry, who had been looking quite pleased up to now, scowled and released the man who, once freed, stood there massaging his neck and shoulders.

"The cops'll be here any minute," Harry said. "I'll be downstairs if you need me." He turned on his heel and left.

The cops did indeed arrive a moment later. They ran a check on the shoplifter, who turned out to have twenty-seven previous convictions, arrested him and took him away.

Before they left, one of the officers took Ted aside. "You better not rough them up like this again. We don't like to take them in when they're bleeding or bruised. There's a lot of paperwork involved. The guy might say we did it. This happens again, we just might decide not to make an arrest."

"One of our guys got a little carried away," said Ted apologetically.

"We got guys like that too," said the cop. "It's a real headache. Tell him you can't leave marks."

Ted was alarmed. Harry had really overreacted. He decided to have a little talk with him. It was a matter of some delicacy, Harry being a Krogstad on his mother's side, but it had to be done, and Karl certainly wouldn't do it. If Karl had his way, they'd be stomping every shoplifter into a pulp out on the loading dock and pitching the broken bodies into the dumpsters.

"Let's increase the frequency on the tape," said Karl.

"All right," said Ted with a shudder. It made him uncomfortable that Galaxy Foods ran a special tape with a subliminal "Thou Shalt Not Steal" message on it under the canned music. The whole thing gave Ted the wim-wams, but Karl Krogstad swore by it.

"Maybe we should add 'an eye for an eye, a tooth for a tooth,'" Karl added.

64

Ted laughed, but stopped when he realized from Karl's expression that the old man wasn't joking. He turned the laugh into a slight cough and left the office.

He found Harry leaning intently at the video-rental counter talking to his sister Louise. When Harry saw Ted approach, he scowled and stomped off. Ted was startled to see Louise's face shiny with tears. She rearranged an errant curl, looked shyly up at Ted and looked away again.

Ted went after Harry, who was now wrestling with a couple of stuck-together carts in the front of the store, and swearing softly under his breath. Harry looked so angry that Ted backed away, deciding to let him cool down before he brought up the subject of vigilantism and gratuitous violence.

He went back to the video department. Louise blinked fiercely and managed to look composed once again, although there were two red spots on her cheeks. "Hi Ted," she said with a brave attempt at a smile.

"Is Harry okay?" said Ted. "He got all bent out of shape about a shoplifter. I'm kind of worried about him."

"He'll be all right," said Louise, glancing over at her brother. "Harry's kind of—intense."

"I guess so," said Ted, who suddenly got the brilliant idea of letting Louise talk to Harry about losing it with shoplifting suspects. Ted liked to get members of the family to keep each other in line if at all possible. "I was afraid he was going to work the shoplifter over. Him and your grandfather."

"Oh, him." Louise wrinkled her nose. "Grandpa's a little irrational on that point."

"Yeah. Well, we can't have anybody beating up members of the public. Harry slammed the guy into some Presto logs, then frog-marched him upstairs to the office—"

"Like a cat," said Louise thoughtfully.

"A cat?" Louise often seemed a little whimsical.

65

"You know. They catch rats and mice and drag them back to their owners for praise."

"Yes. Well, the point is someone better tell Harry he can't just attack these guys. I mean, the procedure is to call the cops."

"I know."

"Maybe you could mention it to Harry. I don't want him in trouble. The cops were upset. I guess he has quite a temper."

"Oh, he's really very sweet," said Louise in the patronizing tone of the older sister. "You don't need to worry about Harry." But she cast a glance over Harry's way and bit her lip, as if she did worry about him herself. Harry was banging away at the carts with abandon.

"Look at him," said Ted. "He still seems angry. I mean, the shoplifter's been dragged away in handcuffs. All we're out is a jar of salsa." Ted suddenly remembered the salsa needed cleaning up in front of the store.

"Oh, but he's not mad at the shoplifter," said Louise, as Ted hustled away to take care of the spill. It was while he was picking the larger shards of glass off the pavement that Ted wondered what Louise meant. He hoped Harry wasn't mad at him. Not after seeing the way he'd smashed the guy's face into the Presto logs. Which reminded him to go over to the stack of logs, find the one with the bloodstain, and remove it from the display.

9

Ginger Jessup had lived in a small, fairly modern condominium on the slope of Queen Anne Hill. The cedar-shaked building was situated at the end of a cul-de-sac. Her unit was on the ground floor, with sliding aluminum doors leading to a small deck.

The manager, a sleepy young man in his late twenties, with tousled hair and shorts and a T-shirt, gave them the key. "Yeah, I heard all about it on the news," he said, above the sound of loud jazz. "We hadn't seen her around, but she took off once in a while." He smoothed down his hair.

"Didn't she usually tell you when she was leaving? Ask you to take in her paper or whatever?" said MacNab.

"She didn't take a paper. And all the mail she ever got was bills and catalogs."

"There's no signs of a struggle or anything in her place," he added.

Lukowski and MacNab looked at each other. "So you've been in her unit since she disappeared?"

"Yeah. When I heard what happened yesterday, I went down and checked it out. I didn't touch anything," he added, padding into the kitchen and peering into his refrigerator, pulling out a carton of milk and taking a swig.

The detectives frowned, and he glanced at them over his milk carton. "The thing is, the owners asked me to make sure everything was okay," he said defensively when he came up for air.

"The owners?"

"Well, Mom and Dad. They're the owners." He wiped his mouth with the back of his hand. "Mom was kind of curious. She came over and we went in there. But it gave Mom the creeps, so she just tiptoed around a little and we left." He gave an embarrassed little laugh.

"You mind keeping out of there until we tell you?" said Lukowski. "And keep anyone else out too, okay?"

"Including Mom," added MacNab.

"Okay."

"When did you see her last?" he continued.

"I can't remember."

"Her fiancé came and picked her up on Saturday the fifth." said Lukowski. "Did you see her since then?"

"Her fiancé?"

"Yeah, she was engaged."

"Which one was she engaged to?" said the manager, hurtling himself into a kitchen chair but not bothering to offer a seat to the two detectives.

"What do you mean, which one?" said MacNab.

"Well, she had a couple of boyfriends that I noticed," he said. "Lately, anyway, seems there were two."

"What did they look like?" said MacNab.

"I don't know. There was a guy with a Camaro and a guy with a Buick. I never saw the guys, just their cars."

"I see."

"Her fiancé must be the guy with the Camaro, right?"

"What makes you say that?" said Lukowski.

The manager looked slightly embarrassed. "Well, the Camaro stayed overnight. And we had a noise complaint a couple of times while the guy was here. The Buick always left around ten or eleven, and things were quiet."

"What kind of a noise complaint?" asked MacNab.

"The unit above her. An older lady. Said she couldn't get to sleep because of the screams."

"Screams?"

"Orgasmic screams," said the manager. "That's what the old lady called them. 'I was young once,' she said, 'but I was always considerate of other people.' That's what she said." He grinned happily at being able to share this information.

"Did you bring it up to Miss Jessup?" said MacNab.

"Hell, no. She always paid her rent on time. Besides, she probably couldn't help it. Mrs. Jacobs is a big whiner, anyway. She's the one that called the cops about the car out in front."

"What car out in front?"

"Didn't you guys already know about that? That Saturday when they say she disappeared, there was a car parked out front for a couple of hours. There was some guy in it and Mrs. Jacobs said he was staking out the place. It must have been a slow night, 'cause the cops showed up and the guy blasted out of here." The manager looked startled. "I figured you guys knew about that."

"Yeah," said MacNab absently, jingling the keys. "We'll talk to Mrs. Jacobs and take a look around."

"Someone stalked her," said Lukowski as they walked through the landscaped grounds to the outside stairs that

69

led to Mrs. Jacobs's apartment. "A police report and everything, and we don't hear a thing about it."

"That manager is a jerk," said MacNab, who never liked anyone very much. "He was just getting up and it's ten o'clock in the morning. If his parents didn't own the place, he'd have to get a real job and he'd probably be shit out of luck. Guys like that really frost me." He glanced around at the landscaping. "Kid should water. Look at those rhodys." MacNab paused thoughtfully. "Either the grocer wasn't banging her or he did a piss-poor job of it," he mused.

Lukowski had been prepared for a frail old lady in cameos, but the manager's definition of old appeared to be mid-forties. Mrs. Jacobs had thick, dark graying hair cut in a chic cut, big hooped earrings, large, liquid brown eyes, and a snubby, shrewd face. Her ample bosom was encased in a sweatshirt that proclaimed A WOMAN NEEDS A MAN LIKE A FISH NEEDS A BICYCLE, and she wore purple sweatpants and house slippers.

"That's right. I called the police," she said, inviting them in to sit on bamboo furniture with tropical cushions. A few large ferns dominated the small living room, and a Siamese cat snoozed by the window. "There was some guy parked outside for about an hour, just staring at the building. It gave me the creeps. I haven't been living alone that long," she explained.

She had not, it appeared, got a license number or the make of the car, which seemed to be either dark blue or black. Neither had she had a good look at its occupant, other than to say he had light hair and looked youngish, muscular, and clean shaven.

"I watched from my window. The police car arrived and the dark car took off and the police car took after it, and that's all I know."

"Did you know Miss Jessup?" asked Lukowski.

"No. I saw her more on those tedious supermarket ads than in person."

70

"Was she a quiet neighbor?" said Lukowski.

Mrs. Jacobs lifted an eyebrow and poked a cigarette into her mouth. "You can hear everything," she said. "And I mean everything." She snapped a disposable lighter and settled back looking pleased with herself.

This was all the entrée Lukowski needed. "The manager said you complained about her passionate screaming."

"That's right. The hair dryer and the aerobics tape, that's one thing, but all that panting and giggling and, well, frankly, screaming, it really got to me. She looked like a slut on those ads, so I wasn't surprised to hear that performance." Mrs. Jacobs sneered. "I suppose the guy or guys bought it all, but meantime, I was trying to get some sleep."

"I see. Did you ever see her, er, guests?"

"No. Frankly, I avoided her. After all, I'd complained to the manager about her, and I thought it would be embarrassing to face her after I'd listened to all that fooling around coming from her place."

Mrs. Jacobs looked suddenly tense. "I suppose I should have called her about that guy parked out in front. I mean, I guess he was staking out her place. He was right under the tree, in front of the entrance to her unit." She rose and went to the window and pointed out. "I even thought, maybe it's some wacko who saw those stupid ads and thinks he's in love or something. But I didn't call. She was home, too."

"She was?" said Lukowski.

"That's right. There was someone in there with her."

"One of the—"

Mrs. Jacobs waved her hand impatiently. "No, it wasn't one of those nights. There were just low voices coming from the living room. For about an hour, I guess."

"Any idea who her guest was?" asked Lukowski.

"No. But something tells me it wasn't social." She frowned.

71

"What makes you say that?" pressed Lukowski, leaning forward.

"I'm not sure," said Mrs. Jacobs thoughtfully. "She had friends over once in a while, and it's different. There's laughing and so forth. And she usually walks back and forth from the kitchen to the living room. You know what I mean?"

"Sure," said MacNab. "Getting them something to eat or a cup of coffee or something."

"That's right," said Mrs. Jacobs. "It was strange. The conversation sounded low and kind of hard, and there was no laughing." She frowned and the detectives were silent a minute because she looked as if she were searching her mind for some detail.

A flicker of triumphant memory crossed her face. "And the stereo wasn't on at first. Usually when she entertained, she had the stereo on. That kind of elevator music, you know? She really didn't have much taste, I don't think. Anyway, it was just this conversation."

"This other person, could you tell if it was a man or a woman?" said MacNab.

"I sort of assumed it was a man, just because she struck me as someone who mostly hung out with men."

Lukowski inadvertently looked down at the sentiment emblazoned on Mrs. Jacobs's chest.

She laughed. "Oh, this. It was a present from a friend of mine. After my husband took off. I guess I sound kind of bitter about Ginger Jessup. It's not women like her who bug me, really. It's the fact that men buy into it so much. I mean look at her. You couldn't even tell what she really looked like underneath all that makeup and stuff. Really, she almost looked like a female impersonator, when you think about it. And that little baby voice. It was all so pathetic. But it worked. That's what's so infuriating about the Gingers of this world."

"I guess she wasn't too popular with a lot of women,"

said MacNab, interjecting a rare personal note. "My wife hated those ads."

"She wasn't really very nice, either," said Mrs. Jacobs. "She always walked past me like I didn't exist. Her mouth kind of turned down and her eyes got kind of cold. That's all right, I guess. But once, I had a man over. A guy I work with. We'd been to the symphony and we came back here for coffee—" Mrs. Jacobs waved her cigarette impatiently, realizing she was explaining more than was necessary. "Anyway, we walked past her in the parking lot, and suddenly, she was friendly and she kind of beamed at us. She was on, you know. It was remarkable. Her face got all shiny and lit up, and I could see it, all of a sudden. What it was they liked about her. She seemed so enthusiastic and vital. I guess she really liked men. Or the attention they gave her anyway, and they thought she liked them."

Ginger's apartment was tidy and presentable. An Exersize bike faced the TV in the living room, and there was a row of fashion magazines in an overlapping line on the glass coffee table. Lukowski stuck his finger in the soil around a large philodendron. Dry.

MacNab opened a small desk and riffled expertly through stacks of papers. "Nothing," he said. "Just bills and some tax stuff. And the usual shoe box full of cancelled checks. Let's take them and have a look."

"Okay," said Lukowski absently. There were no personal touches besides a refrigerator magnet shaped like a cat and holding up a pot holder. The refrigerator had a container of cottage cheese, a half bottle of white wine, some ketchup, and a brownish head of lettuce. The freezing compartment had a stack of frozen diet dinners. He pulled open the dishwasher. There was a cereal bowl there and a couple of glasses. One of them had a ring of mold running around the inside.

The bedroom had a red velvet flocked headboard, a dressing table full of bottles and jars, and a long closet with louvred doors. On a chair was a collection of dresses. One was black satin with narrow straps. Another was blue crepe with a rhinestone buckle. The third was white and slinky. Over a chair was a black-and-white polka-dot number.

"Couldn't decide what to wear," said Lukowski.

MacNab nodded. He pulled open a dresser drawer and lifted up a transparent black-and-red teddy. He whistled. "Guess this was her screaming outfit."

Lukowski snorted. "That screaming was probably a good act." He opened the closet. There were a lot of clothes, all perfectly organized. There was also a collection of high-heeled pumps in bright colors, and a couple of pairs of tennis shoes.

MacNab shrugged. "As long as it was a good act, who cares?" he said, eyeing the garment rather wistfully. "Wonder why she didn't put on an act for the grocer."

"Didn't have to. He was already going to marry her," said Lukowski, hovering at the bedside table. Here he found a copy of *Cosmopolitan* and an address book. There was also an answering machine with a red light on. Lukowski pushed the button. "Hi, Honey, it's me." It was Karl Krogstad's voice. "Is everything okay? I have to talk to you. It's Saturday at two in the morning. Why aren't you home, honeybunch? Call me."

Karl Krogstad had left eighteen of them, each with an increasing degree of desperation. "I hope you aren't mad at me, sweetiepie. Call me. I'm so worried," was the last one.

The only other two messages, somewhere in the middle of the tape, consisted of one hang up and one call from a clothing store. "That orange spandex jumpsuit you ordered is in," it said. "We can hold it for you for three days."

"She won't be needing it where she's going," said Lukowski with a big sigh.

74

"Camaro didn't call," said MacNab. "Interesting."

Lukowski flipped through the address book and put it in his pocket, then stepped into the bathroom. There was a hair dryer, a magnifying mirror on a flexible arm sprouting from the wall, a rattan shelf full of makeup, nail polish, cotton balls, Q-Tips, a curling iron, and, like two specimens in a petri dish, a pair of false eyelashes floating in a little dish.

MacNab looked over Lukowski's shoulder and sighed. "She worked out, she read magazines, she bought clothes. And she had those two guys. That's it."

"Oh, but she had a hobby," said Lukowski, drifting back into the bedroom and browsing among the perfume bottles on her dresser. "Look at this. She had a swizzle stick collection." He pointed to a brandy snifter full of them.

"After we work the address book, if we still can't find Camaro, we work these. Maybe someone saw them out together at one of these places. She was famous. She was the Galaxy Foods girl. She'd be remembered."

Later, when the detectives had boxed up some personal records and carried them out to their car, Lukowski went back to the manager's apartment.

"Come in," yelled the young man who was now ensconced in front of the television, watching a game show. He turned to Lukowski with one arm hooked over the sofa. "Yeah?"

"Listen," said Lukowski, "when you were talking about her boyfriends, you said there were two at the moment. Is there anyone she might have stopped seeing recently? Before the Camaro and the Buick?"

"I don't think so," said the manager. "I can't remember."

"Well, think about it, and let us know," said Lukowski. "We'll be in touch. I'm leaving my card on your kitchen table in case anything comes up."

"Okay." The man turned back to the tube.

"We'll hang onto these keys for a while, if you don't mind," said Lukowski.

"That's okay," he said. "I have my own key. Those are hers."

Lukowski looked down at the keys in his hand. There was a car key on the ring next to the apartment key. He felt like an idiot for not noticing that before.

"So how did you get them?" said Lukowski.

"When Mom and I went in there, they were on the coffee table," he said.

10

◆

Ted stepped back and surveyed his handiwork. He had finished draping a large, shiny-lipped photograph of Ginger Jessup with a tasteful ribbon of black crepe paper. Underneath, in thick black type were the words GINGER JESSUP—GALAXY FOODS SPOKESPERSON. THE GALAXY FOODS FAMILY MOURNS HER PASSING. Ted had pasted this strip across the bottom of the picture, obscuring an inch or so of cleavage that seemed disrespectful considering the circumstances.

Karl Krogstad had insisted that Ted come up with some tribute to the dead pitchwoman. A "fitting in-store memorial" was what Karl had asked for, and this was the best Ted could do, although he imagined the old man would have preferred to have her lying in state in the store like Eva Perón or Lenin, the way he'd gone on about it.

The whole arrangement was propped up on an easel near the service desk next to a large sign describing the store's check cashing policy. It still needed a little something, so Ted swung by floral and grabbed a pot of white mums in green foil with a white ribbon and plunked it down in front. He sighed deeply and checked his watch. The funeral was scheduled for that afternoon, and he still had the weekend scheduling to do as soon as he came back. Knowing the day would be tight, he'd brought his dark suit to work with him. He wondered if he should change now.

Louise sidled up to him and raised an eyebrow at his display. "Touching," she said out of the side of her mouth, crossing her arms and shifting her weight to one leg and bending it so she sank an inch or so.

"Your grandfather wanted me to put something together," said Ted, feeling like an idiot. The little display looked so hokey. "Some memorial or other. It's the best I could come up with."

"How about, 'In fond memory of Ginger Jessup, Galaxy Foods honors all manufacturers' coupons at double the face value for a period of mourning.' "

"Offer not valid on tobacco or alcohol items," added Ted with a smirk. "He's upset, but not that upset." Double couponing was one of Karl Krogstad's pet peeves.

"I was wondering if you could give me a ride to the funeral," said Louise. She added defensively "I don't really want to go. I'm just doing it for Grandpa."

"Sure, I'll be glad to," said Ted, reflecting on the fact that it was probably a lot less of a chore for the family to show up at the funeral than it would have been to appear at the wedding. In fact, the Krogstads were probably rather cheerful about the change in ceremonies.

"Meet me in video in about an hour," said Louise, checking her watch.

As Ted swung by the front end, he noticed lines forming. He opened another checkstand. "I can help you over here," Ted said to a woman with two small children. Her cart was piled high. Ted gestured over to Jason, who was just coming in from the lot with a bunch of carts. "You wanna help me bag over here?" he said.

"Paper or plastic?" said Jason, as Ted started to scan.

"Plastic," said the woman, fumbling in her purse. "I use them to line the garbage can."

Jason was getting to be a pretty fast bagger, noted Ted with approval. He'd already filled four bags. His face was twisted in concentration.

"I've got coupons," said the customer, waggling a wad of them about an inch thick.

Ted experienced a sinking feeling. This woman was a professional coupon shopper. The kind who appeared on TV news shows and in magazine features where some beleaguered checker rang up a total of two hundred dollars and then backed out the coupons and the customer had to pay seven dollars and twenty-one cents.

Even with bar codes on the coupons, it was a checker's nightmare. First you scanned the items, then you scanned the coupons. The problem was visually verifying she'd actually bought all the products. And, the woman had craftily waited until four bags were already filled before she'd mentioned she had coupons. Ted smelled a rat, and decided to check all the expiration dates like a hawk.

"Ted," said Jason in a worried tone "I gotta talk to you."

"Yeah, okay" he said to Jason. To the customer he said sternly "You hand me the coupon as I ring up each item. You should have told me you had coupons before I started." The woman's face set in a frown. Behind her, other customers looked antagonistic. Ted flipped on the

79

intercom. "We'll need another checker," he said, knowing he was hunkering in for a long haul.

"It's real important," said Jason.

"It'll have to wait," said Ted, grimly peering out over the counter. "So that's the Tide? The coupon says it's good on liquid Tide detergent only." A note of triumph crept into his voice. He sent Jason back to exchange the item. Ted wanted her to know he wasn't going to fool around. He hadn't seen her here before, and he'd just as soon she took her business elsewhere. If he made it too tough, she would. He made a big deal of scrutinizing the top couple of coupons and looking dubious. "You sure about all your expiration dates?" He clicked his tongue.

"They're all good," said the woman huffily. "And here's for the coffee," she said. "It went into one of those bags at the beginning."

"I'm sorry," said Ted with a killer smile. "I don't even have to check the tape, because we don't carry that brand. No one does, west of the Mississippi." He tossed the coupon back. Okay. Now it was out in the open. She was a chiseler. He was pleased he'd tripped her up on the coffee. It was a whole dollar off.

He had her on the defensive now, and riffled through a few more coupons. Her children were beginning to whine restlessly. The boy was doing flips on the chrome bar between checkstands. "Watch it," said Ted sharply, "or you'll crack your little skull. Ball Park franks is expired. And so is the free milk and bananas with Rice Krispies. Sorry."

He started to hand back the offending coupons, then crumpled them slowly up before her eyes. "I may as well throw them away," he said sadistically. "They're no good."

Jason came huffing back with a plastic bottle of detergent. "That's not right," Ted said irritably. You brought Cheer. We needed Tide."

Much to Ted's amazement, Jason grew red in the face and tears came into his eyes. "Is Cheer okay?" said Ted to the customer. He'd make it good later. Jason seemed to be falling apart, and Ted didn't know quite what to do about it.

"Yeah, if you let me have the Ball Park franks," she said with a smirk.

"Forget it," said Ted. Try to do someone a favor and they whomp all over you. "Tide, please," he said to Jason, who was now blinking back tears. "And take a break as soon as you bring it back," he said. "Are you okay?" he whispered.

"I gotta talk to you," said Jason, biting his lip.

"All right, all right. Let me just get this buttoned up." Ted rang up the total on a cartload of bags. Then he scanned the coupons. After a barrage of electronic blips, he got the revised total. "Twelve dollars and seventy-one cents, please." He kept any hint of astonishment or admiration out of his voice. These women got some kind of an adrenaline rush when they heard how low the total was. He wasn't going to do anything to contribute to her satisfaction. She paid with exact change from a tiny coin purse and Jason showed up with the Tide and wheeled her cart out.

Ted didn't have the heart to whip out the "checkstand closed" sign just now. The next customer, a young girl, had been waiting so patiently.

Ted watched Jason wheeling the coupon lady's cart to the exit from the corner of his eye. What was the matter with the kid, anyway? Ted grabbed the intercom and barked into it "Where's that checker?" As soon as he was relieved, he'd follow Jason into the break room and find out what was behind his adolescent sulks.

"I guess that lady saves a lot," said the next customer. Ted seethed inwardly and repressed the impulse to say, "Why doesn't she get a life?"

Ted knew his views on these women—who spent hours soaking off labels, maintaining them in filing systems and mailing them to clearing houses in the Midwest for coupons—bordered on the irrational. But from his point of view, they were leeches on society. They saved a lot, but a real job would pay as much and contribute something worthwhile to the world. Meanwhile, because they were willing to chisel and nickel and dime it, and take advantage of a serious and outmoded flaw in the distribution system, other shoppers paid more for groceries and subsidized them. If Ted were king, he had thought many times to himself, the first thing he would do would be to issue a proclamation banning all grocery couponing.

A relief checker arrived, and Ted, abandoning his disturbing ruminations about the evils of couponing, handed over the checkstand and went after Jason.

He found him alone in the break room, sucking on a Dr Pepper.

"What's up?" he said.

"I don't know," said Jason, shrugging. "This thing with Ginger Jessup has got me all weirded out. I was wondering if I could have a couple of days off."

"I suppose so," said Ted, slightly bemused.

"People get killed on TV all the time," said Jason.

"Yeah," said Ted. "But it's different in real life." Great, he thought to himself. Maybe the whole staff would snap and they'd have to bring in grief counselors or something.

"You think the cops'll figure out who did it?"

Ted had wondered about that himself, and he didn't know the answer, but to sound reassuring, he said, "Oh, probably. Ginger was kind of famous in her own way. They'll probably work pretty hard to find out who did it."

"Think they'll ask us all a bunch of questions, like on TV?"

"I guess so. Just hammer away until they get a break."

Jason stared into his Dr Pepper. "I hate all this."

"What was it you wanted to talk to me about?" Ted said. He reminded himself Jason was just a kid. Jason's powerful physique made it easy to forget, but right now, hunched over, head down, Jason looked about twelve years old.

"Nothing. It's no big deal. I just got upset."

"I know it's real disturbing," Ted said gently.

"I can't believe she was killed." Jason screwed up his face and tears appeared once more.

"Maybe we can talk later. After the funeral." Ted was puzzled. As far as he knew, Jason had only met Ginger once, when he parked her car the night of the party.

"Are you scared there's a killer loose?" he said.

Jason looked up rather defiantly. "Hell no," he said. "I'm not scared."

But scared was exactly what Jason seemed to be.

11

♦

As he went back up to the office to change into the dark suit he'd last worn for Ginger Jessup's engagement party, Ted decided he'd have to corner Jason later and find out what was on the kid's mind. He'd keep an eye on the rest of the staff for signs of emotional wear and tear, too. And he left himself a note to reschedule around Jason.

He sighed and wondered if Louise would think it was tacky to wear his clip-on polyester uniform tie to the funeral. It was the only black tie he owned.

When he went back down to the video department, Louise managed, by arching her spine slightly and tossing her heavy hair, to make something sensuous out of untying the strings behind her back and insinuating her lanky body out of her apron. Ted sighed. Maybe it was just his imagination, but he didn't think so.

In his car, Louise made herself at home, riffling through his tapes, before selecting one and jamming it proprietorially into the stereo. "You're pretty smart. In fact, you're very smart. Tell me who you think killed Ginger," she said, as jazz piano filled the car.

"I haven't the faintest idea," said Ted, absolutely determined not to touch the topic. Gossiping with the Krogstads was a bad move.

"I'm afraid it's one of us," said Louise solemnly. He turned to look at her and her big gray-blue eyes looked huge. "God, I hope it's Lance."

Ted rather liked that idea himself. Lance was a nasty piece of work, all right. He could see him pushing his thumbs into Ginger's throat. Why he would do so wasn't, however, entirely clear. As far as anyone could tell, Lance was still the fair-haired boy with the old man, and he had a lifetime of smarming ahead of him. He might have to share the little gold mine with the widow, but he'd still have a free hand.

"He's out of town. Skiing," said Ted.

"That's what his father says," said Louise with a little smile of triumph. "But then Uncle Junior also says Aunt Ellen is in some funny farm in California."

"Isn't she?" said Ted, startled.

Louise looked proud to be offering some special knowledge. "She's been spotted at the Liz Claiborne store doing some heavy, heavy shopping."

"The Liz Claiborne store?" said Ted.

"You know, the designer. Not that great for me. More for the petite woman. Aunt Ellen's only five-three. How tall do you think I am?"

"I don't know," said Ted impatiently. "Didn't we already talk about this? You're just a little shorter than I am."

86

"I think I'm taller."

Ted's voice rose a little. "Look," he said, "I wouldn't really care if you were, but you're not." He refrained from adding his usual sally about height being irrelevant when two people were lying down.

"When was this?" said Ted.

"When was what?"

"When was Aunt Ellen sighted?"

"Oh. Yesterday. A friend of my mother's ran into her. She was charging up a storm. She always does that when she's pissed off at Uncle Junior. Goes crazy with the plastic."

Ted glanced at her profile. She had a cute nose. "I wonder if there was anything to it." he said.

"To what?"

"Oh, I hate to pry. I don't mean to get into your family dynamics or anything." He sighed.

Louise reacted just as he'd meant her to. "Come on. What is it?"

"That scene at Ginger's party. When your Aunt Ellen—" he trailed off. "Oh, never mind."

"You mean do you think Junior and Ginger were—"

"I was kind of curious."

Louise shrugged. "We'll probably never know. It's certainly possible. Uncle Junior's pretty sleazy. Spends all his time hanging around that sports bar in the mall picking up barflies. Ginger would have been a step up for him.

"Anyway," she said, flicking her hair back over her shoulder, "what's wrong with Lance as the killer?"

"I don't think you should make any reckless accusations," said Ted. "After all, he is your cousin. Let the police handle this."

Actually, the more Ted thought about it, the more he liked the idea. Lance serving twenty to life in Walla Walla State Prison should make life considerably easier around the store. He allowed himself a small smile.

"But why would he have wanted to?" said Ted.

"Any of us would have wanted to," said Louise. "She could have ended up with the store."

"Is your family that ruthless?" said Ted, rather shocked.

"You've met Lance," said Louise.

"Okay, maybe he's a slime, but do you think he'd be crazy enough to kill someone just because they might inherit the store? Someday?"

"No, probably not," said Louise, sounding terribly disappointed. "It was just a thought."

They turned into the gravel parking lot of the church, just in time to see Karl Krogstad being helped out of a long black limousine by Lance. Lance was wearing a shiny black silk suit, but it hung awkwardly. Ted gave him a second look and realized why. Lance's empty sleeve was tucked in his jacket pocket and his arm was in a stiff white plaster cast.

"Looks like Lance had a spill on the slopes," said Ted as he yanked up on the emergency brake.

"We'll have to find out when he got that cast," said Louise with a gleam in her eye. "It said on the news she'd been dead less than twenty-four hours when they found her."

"I was thinking the same thing," said Ted. "I don't see how he could have strangled her with that thing on his arm."

◆

"Ginger Jessup, who we're buryin' today," began the minister in a crackery twang, "was blessed by the Lord with a *beautiful* body."

Ted cringed and hoped no one would have the bad taste to shout out an "amen" at this point. The church was grim—a concrete block oblong with rows of folding chairs. Some narrow aluminum-framed windows let in a sickly light. The minister, a rangy, florid man who'd introduced himself as Pastor Bob before he started, wore a shiny green suit and a string tie. This, thought Ted, was Protestantism at its absolute tackiest.

"Yes, friends. She was a beautiful woman. No doubt about it." Pastor Bob closed his eyes and paused as if contemplating the dead woman's good looks, and Karl Krogstad let out with a sob. "Maybe some men *lusted* after that body," said the minister.

"No kidding," said Louise in a whisper out of the side of her mouth.

"And maybe some women were *jealous* because of it."

"He got that right," Ted whispered back to her.

"But now that our little sister Ginger is in heaven with the Lord Jesus and all who've been called to him, and free of those *earthly* ties," Pastor Bob rushed his words now and raised the volume, like a TV preacher, *"she can bask in the pure love of Jesus. He doesn't want her body, no friends, he wants her soul."*

The sermon conjured up in Ted's mind a rather shocking picture of Jesus Christ holding Ginger's hand and assuring her he was interested only in her soul while glancing down at those fabulous breasts. He wished Pastor Bob would stop talking about Ginger's body in conjunction with Jesus. It seemed in bad taste.

Tuning out the eulogy, Ted glanced discreetly around the church. Because he and Louise were seated at the side of the church, and the metal folding chairs were arranged in a U shape, he could get a look at most of the mourners.

A lot of people from the store seemed to be there. All the department managers, anyway. They weren't stupid.

There was also a contingent of other Galaxy Foods operators, and a sprinkling of executives from United Independent Grocers. Ted also recognized Mel, the Galaxy Foods ad manager, in a dark tweed jacket, and wondered if he felt bad he'd made that joke about a cup of coffee and a blow job from Ginger Jessup.

The Krogstads were all there too, of course, except for Ellen, who was presumably out shopping. Louise's mother sat with her husband Stan, looking politely up at Pastor Bob, while her husband just looked uncomfortable. Louise's brother Harry sat staring at his shoes and scowling. Karl Krogstad was visibly weeping. He was flanked by his son Junior and his grandson Lance. Karl seemed to be listing over towards Lance, as if leaning on him.

The rest of the mourners were an odd collection. A pair of aerobicized women with big hairdos sat over to one side. One of them was chewing gum. A tanned middle-aged man with silver hair and an expensive suit sat alone. Near the front was a large, sixtyish woman in a spongy-looking green polyester dress. She was crying and smiling up at Pastor Bob at the same time, her face simultaneously blotchy and beatific. She was supported by two similar ladies on either side.

Ted tuned back in as Pastor Bob continued. "Her life took her far from us. Far from this humble congregation. Ginger was on TV, and even took a trip down to Hollywood. She mighta been a big star if she hadn't a-been cut down and called home. But Ginger's mom, our sister in Christ, Shirley"—here the minister extended a hand towards the woman who'd been crying—"raised her up to believe in the Lord Jesus and to accept him as her personal savior, and so, even in the glamorous world where she lived, Ginger took a part of us with her, and it's a good thing she did, because now, she'll have to account for herself, no matter how famous she was here on earth, as we all will some day no matter how big we get, *you better believe it.*" Pastor Bob's tone had become threatening and he shook his finger at the congregation and frowned at them.

"You better believe she wasn't going to have this hick marry her," whispered Louise. "If he's even licensed by the state to perform weddings." She shuddered.

In the back of the church, detectives Lukowski and Mac-

Nab sat impassively. It occurred to Lukowski that the ceremony had nothing to do with Ginger's own religious views. Her condominium hadn't turned up a Bible or anything like that. Just the collected works of Kahlil Gibran and a Jonathan Livingston Seagull poster.

MacNab leaned over to him. "I bet this poor jerk wishes he could've been on TV and made himself some big bucks. Instead, he sees Ginger pitching groceries. I bet it really fried him. Maybe he got so upset he strangled her. Heh-heh-heh."

Lukowski frowned and faced forward. He wished MacNab wouldn't talk in church, even if it did look like a garage.

After the service, Pastor Bob invited the mourners to take some refreshments in the church basement. As the mourners filed out, the two detectives lingered. "I say let's go right over to the store and start grilling everyone," said MacNab. "We'll get more out of the help when the family's at the wake."

12

◆

As soon as Ted returned to the store, he sensed things were out of hand. First of all, there were too many carts out in the parking lot. A bad sign. He pushed a couple of them inside with him and was confronted with a jam-up at the front end. "Get some more checkers," he said sharply, as he walked by on his way to the office. He'd been right to forgo the reception and see what was happening here.

In produce, he noticed a heap of lemons on the floor and a few empty plastic bag rolls. He frowned and headed for the swinging doors that led to the produce area. When he pushed open the door, he was horrified to discover a food fight in progress. Ted, in his younger days stocking shelves after hours, was known to have been involved in a few himself, but always on the night shift—never during peak traffic hours. Two produce guys were throwing tomatoes at each other, and a young woman, giggling and shrieking, was covering her head and ducking, caught in the cross fire.

"Very funny," said Ted. "Clean this mess up." He bent over and picked up a squashed tomato. "Come on, guys. Not the Romas at eighty-nine cents a pound," he said with dismay. "Can't you use the salad tomatoes on special at forty-nine?"

He slapped his forehead. "What am I saying? Don't throw any of this stuff around! Mr. Krogstad would raise holy hell if he knew you were contributing to in-store shrink like this. And by the way, there's spilled lemons on the selling floor and you need more plastic bags. Get it right, will you?"

He pushed angrily at the swinging doors. Everything was probably slack all over the store with the department managers and the Krogstads all at the church. Not that the latter were particularly effectual leaders, but their presence did seem to put the brakes on truly outrageous behavior.

As Ted walked past deli, he noticed one of Marvella's greasy-looking young assistants licking a spoon with which he'd just stirred up a batch of potato salad.

"Where are you putting that spoon now?" hissed Ted. "Back in the potato salad?"

"In the sink," he said nervously.

"Don't you ever touch anything around here with anything besides your hands again," said Ted. "And while you're at it, wash your hands. Who knows where they've been."

Ted walked on, scowling.

In the office, he discovered that the two detectives, MacNab and Lukowski, had comandeered Mr. Krogstad's private office. Through the glass door he could see the back

of Jason's head and his big shoulders, and settled in opposite him, behind the big desk, the two detectives. He resented the way they'd made themselves at home. Next
thing, they'd be telling him how to run the store.

Ted had planned to make a few bad check calls, then go
over the schedule. He sat down and noted with chagrin a
pile of pink message slips. Before he had a chance to tackle
them, the phone rang and the caller identified himself as
Bud Wyatt of Wyatt Optical, and the phone book recycling
committee chairman of the North End Business Owners'
Association. "We'll be bringing the bin in this afternoon,"
he said.

"What bin?" Ted squinted at some of the phone messages. A lot of them seemed to be personal calls for employees. He weeded these out and threw them in the
wastebasket. Work was piling up too fast to run an answering service for the checkers.

"One of the owners authorized it. Stan Hamilton."

Ted refrained from pointing out that Louise's stepfather
was not one of the owners, and braced himself. Stan Hamilton was notorious for offering the services of the store to
any community group. He was always schmoozing around
lunch meetings, trying to sell real estate to a lot of losers
who spent too much time at meetings and not enough
running their businesses.

"It shouldn't take up more than a couple of parking
spaces."

Ted frowned. Parking was tight as it was.

"And we really look forward to having you at that softball
tourney, too. To be honest, we're kind of short on partici-
pants, so maybe you guys could have two teams."

"What softball tourney?"

"Your boss says you'll be fielding a team for the disabled
children's fund-raiser." The man sounded slightly exasperated, as if Ted should be up to speed.

"I'll talk to Stan about it," said Ted irritably.

95

"Well, the registration fee is due now. And we have to get the team outfitted with T-shirts. They're fifteen dollars apiece. Have you got the list of sizes? They have to be silk-screened tomorrow." Wyatt clicked his tongue. "You better talk to Stan. He said his people were all set to go."

"There's been a death in the family," said Ted, hoping this would put the man at bay. He was tempted to tell him to go grind some lenses and stop bothering other people with all his good works. "Stan is still at the services."

The caller's voice switched to a sympathetic tone. "Oh, I see," he said. "It must be Stan's father-in-law who passed away. Stan told me he was very ill and wasn't expected to last too long. I guess it's a blessing when their health has been so bad."

"Mr. Krogstad is still with us," said Ted. "His fiancée died. Didn't you read about it in the papers?"

"Oh, I see," said the caller. "But I thought he had a bad heart. Stan said so."

Ted was tempted to ask the caller to call Mr. Krogstad's doctor if he wanted a full medical report.

Just then, Jason emerged from the office, flanked by the two detectives.

"Jason's gonna call his mom" said MacNab.

A quick glance at Jason revealed that he was scared. He looked even worse than he had in the break room the last time they'd talked. His face was kind of crumpled and pale, like a little kid's. Ted was shocked at the helplessness he saw there.

"Call me back later," he said to the man from the North End Business Owners' Association.

"I need some answers right now," said the man.

"Stan will call you back," said Ted, hanging up. To Lukowski, who seemed like the more intelligent of the two cops, he said "What's going on here?"

MacNab answered. "Jason wants to use the phone."

"What is it, Jason?" said Ted.

96

"They want to arrest me," said Jason.

"No we don't," said MacNab impatiently. "We just want to take him down to Juvenile and ask him a few more questions."

"What about?"

MacNab glared at Ted, and Lukowski seemed to be observing Jason coolly, as if gauging his mental state.

"They want to give me a polygraph test," said Jason, his shoulders stooping and beginning to shudder.

"Wait a minute," said Ted firmly. "You're scaring him." He put an arm around Jason. "What's the matter, guy?"

"They want to call my mom."

"We just want to ask the boy a few questions," said Mac-Nab impatiently.

"Let me talk to him," said Ted, guiding Jason away from the two men protectively. "What is it, Jason? What was it you wanted to tell me earlier?"

He regretted it instantly. MacNab perked up.

"Look," said Ted rather desperately, "let me talk to him. He's a sensitive kid."

Lukowski shrugged. Rather theatrically, Ted thought. In fact, the whole scene seemed rather theatrical. Like something out of a cheap movie. Just the thing to rattle Jason.

To his surprise, the detectives let him haul Jason back into Krogstad's office. Perhaps it was part of their little drama. The whole thing made Ted angry.

He kicked the door shut behind them.

"What's going on?" he said.

"I followed her," said Jason. "I followed her home that night. She was so pretty. I just wanted to be near her."

"Damn," said Ted. "Did you tell them that?"

"Yeah. Sort of."

"Did you—did you hurt her?"

"No!" Jason shouted it out. "Nothing like that. I just followed her."

MacNab came into the office. "Come on, Jason," he

97

said. "Let's tell your mom you're going down to Twelfth and Alder."

Ted knew Jason's mom. A tired forty year old who looked sixty and spent her life sucking on beers and trying to collect support from Jason's long gone father. He didn't think she could handle this.

"Are you arresting him?" said Ted.

"No."

"You want to polygraph him?"

"Jason jumped the gun a little there," said MacNab.

"We just suggested it as a possibility," said Lukowski gently. He gave Jason a little smile. The old hot and cold routine, thought Ted contemptuously.

"You don't have to go with them unless they arrest you," said Ted. "Jason, tell them the truth. Make it sweet and simple and tell them now."

"I followed her home. I parked outside her house and sat in my car. And I saw the guy. That's all." said Jason.

"What guy?" said Ted, fascinated.

"We'd appreciate your keeping our talk confidential, Jason," said Lukowski. "It's safer for everyone."

"Are you finished with him?" said Ted.

"For now we are," said MacNab.

"Can I ask you to finish your shift," said Ted in level, calm tones he hoped would somehow soothe Jason.

The boy's lip trembled a little.

"I need you," said Ted. "We're shorthanded." It would do the kid good, Ted thought, to work. "The lot's full of carts."

"Okay," said Jason.

"Run along," said MacNab with a sigh.

"He's a good kid," said Ted after Jason had left. "Really he is." He felt like a jerk saying it. Probably these guys had met a million good kids who'd gone berserk somehow.

MacNab curled his lip.

98

"Is there anything more I can do for you gentlemen?" said Ted.

"As a matter of fact," said Lukowski, "there is. We're talking to everyone here at the store. Trying to get the big picture. Is now a good time?"

"Why not?" said Ted, who found himself secretly thrilled. Maybe he could get an idea about the drift of the investigation by the questions they asked.

They stepped into Karl Krogstad's office, but Ted sat behind the desk, indicating guest chairs for the two policemen.

The questions were straightforward and simple. No, Ted hadn't met Ginger Jessup before the engagement party at the Moon Temple Garden. Yes, he'd noticed there'd been kind of a dustup between Ellen Krogstad and her future stepmother-in-law. No, he had no idea what it was about. "No direct knowledge, anyway," said Ted, correcting himself.

"Well, what did you find out later about that?" said Lukowski.

Ted shrugged. "There was a lot of gossip around the store," he said. He wasn't sure he wanted to drag out all the Krogstads' dirty linen.

"This is a police investigation," said Lukowski slowly and with an intent look in his grayish eyes. "We are investigating a homicide. We're not interested in a lot of gossip for its own sake, but we do want to know what was happening here, and we think you should tell us."

Ted nodded. "Fair enough," he said. "The word was Ellen accused Ginger of having slept with her husband."

Ted could tell the police had already heard this. "Karl Krogstad, Junior, right?" said MacNab.

"Right."

"Do you have any reason to believe that was true?" said Lukowski.

"No."

99

"We understand there was a shoplifting incident here a few days ago," Lukowski continued.

"We have a lot of that," said Ted.

MacNab cut in. "We understand young Harry McDonald got a little carried away. Roughed up the suspect."

"Yeah. Well, Harry's kind of short-tempered. He hates shoplifters. Just like Mr. Krogstad."

"Would you say he has a pretty bad temper? Is he a violent person?" said Lukowski.

"Not violent enough to strangle Ginger Jessup," said Ted. "Not unless she was shoplifting."

Lukowski nodded. "I see. To your knowledge, did anyone see Ginger Jessup during the week after the party before her body was discovered?"

"No. Mr. Krogstad was looking for her. I know that."

"You mean Karl? The old man?"

"That's right."

"Maybe you can tell us how someone might have put the body inside that bin without being noticed. When this store is open twenty-four hours a day."

"We closed for a week. We were remodeling."

"I see. And who had a key?"

"We don't use keys much, being open twenty-four hours every day of the year except Christmas. We actually had trouble coming up with one for the contractors, but we found one in the office, in a desk drawer. It used to be on a hook behind the office door.

"And there must be a couple floating around from before. Karl has one. And Junior. And I do. I think Leonard LeBlanc had one, because he always comes in early to set up his seafood case. I think produce has one, because they trim produce all night long. And maybe the meat manager. There might be more."

Ted shrugged. "Sorry I'm a little vague about it. It just never comes up."

"I see," said Lukowski. "All right, let me ask you a little

bit about the family's reaction to Ginger Jessup. Do you think they were happy about Mr. Krogstad marrying her?"

"Probably not," said Ted. "She was a lot younger, and in a family business like this, you're not just getting an in-law, you're getting a partner. They might well have resented her."

"I see," said Lukowski. "Well, thank you for your time. We'll be in touch."

"What about Jason?" said Ted. "Is he a suspect?"

"He's a person of interest to the investigation," said MacNab.

"He's just a kind of goofy kid," said Ted. "I can't believe he followed her home. He's never done anything like that before. Girls seem to make him nervous."

"Yeah?" said MacNab, managing to imply in one syllable that Jason was some kind of a sexual psychopath. "Did he have a key to this place?"

"No."

"But he probably could find one," said Lukowski.

"I suppose so." Ted frowned. "But that would be stupid, wouldn't it? To put a body here? It connects the murderer with this store. It doesn't make sense."

"It doesn't make sense to strangle people, either," said Lukowski. "Murderers don't think logically. If they did, they wouldn't run around killing people."

13

◆

The two detectives rose, and Ted saw them out. A minute later Junior and Lance Krogstad came up to the office.

"Grandpa's taking the day off," Lance announced. "He asked me to come by and make sure everything was under control."

"It's under control," said Ted. He glanced down at Lance's cast. "You broke your arm, I see."

Lance smiled a devil-may-care smile. "Skiing up in Canada. Whistler. There was some fantastic white powder up there. I'm glad I got in a few good runs before this happened."

"Tough break," said Ted. "Guess you were taking it a little faster than you should have."

"Hell no," said Junior. "Lance is fantastic on skis."

"Some clown ran into me," said Lance. "Knocked me down. I got my arm all twisted up around my pole and then I fell on it."

"Guess we can't use you as a checker," said Ted.

Lance curled his lip. "Actually, I wasn't planning to do anything like that anyway. A good overview of the store's management practices was what I had in mind to start with."

"We all pitch in checking from time to time," said Ted. "Even your grandfather." Actually, the old man hated scanners and said all the art had gone out of checking since their introduction a decade ago, but he still helped out once in a while when he was needed.

"Yeah," chuckled Lance. "Grandpa's quite a character, isn't he, Dad?"

"That's right," said Junior absently. He had installed himself on the sofa and was leafing through a copy of *Progressive Grocer* without much enthusiasm. Ted figured he was putting in a half hour or so until the cocktail hour began at his favorite bar around the corner.

"Your grandfather is a good businessman who never forgot that the customer is what makes the store work," said Ted, irritated. He knew he should back off and cut Lance some slack. There wasn't any point in alienating him. The thing was, Lance was too stupid to know when he was being insulted.

"So what's been happening while I've been gone?" said Lance.

"We've been selling groceries, same as always," said Ted. What did he mean "what's been happening?" thought Ted. He didn't know enough to know what it was he wanted to know. "Excuse me Lance, I've got to check up on a few things."

"I think I'll just follow you around for a while," said Lance. "Get a handle on what it is you do around here."

104

Ted's heart sank. He'd been planning to find Jason, corner him and see what the boy had told the police. Most important, he wanted to know what Jason had meant when he said "I saw the guy."

"Great idea, Lance," he said. "But you know, there's something I wish you'd handle first."

"What's that?" said Lance, leaning back and looking casual but interested.

"Well, Stan's got us signed up for some community service-type activities with the North End Business Owners' Association. I wish you'd nail down the details. Make sure our corporate presence is shown to best advantage at these events." Ted rummaged around the desk and found the number of Mr. Wyatt, the phone book recycling chairman.

"I'll take care of that," said Lance importantly, striding over to the phone.

"And while you're at it," added Ted, dipping quickly into the wastebasket while Lance's back was turned, "you might get back to some of these people." Ted retrieved the phone messages he'd jettisoned earlier. "Find out what they want. Some of these may be personal calls to employees. Maybe you should tell them our policy on employee phone calls."

"Which is . . ." began Lance.

"Take a look at it in the employee manual," said Ted, slamming down a green loose-leaf binder in front of Lance. "You may want to review some of those phone policies while you're at it."

Lance nodded thoughtfully.

"I know you want to do that management overview," said Ted sympathetically, wondering exactly what a management overview entailed, and not liking the sound of it, "but there are some key decisions that should be made now."

"We've got to think pro-actively," said Lance with a thoughtful frown.

"I agree with you completely," said Ted.

"Glad to hear it, guy" said Lance, sitting down in front

of the phone and assuming a junior executive posture at the desk. Ted congratulated himself on a little pro-active strategy himself. Not only would he keep Lance out of his hair with a few perfectly useless tasks, he'd also set it up so Lance could alienate the staff by hassling them about phone calls. Unhappy employees could do a lot to slow Lance down. There was no need for Ted to take him on all by himself.

As Ted left he heard Lance, his voice lowered an octave, in an attempt to sound adult, asking for Mr. Wyatt. It reminded Ted that something about Wyatt's conversation had struck him as odd. What was it? He'd been interrupted by the detectives grilling Jason.

Ted flew down the stairs and went in search of Jason. He found him out in the lot, slamming down the door on a Volvo station wagon, while a young matron in orange jogging gear simpered at him, ignoring her screaming children in the backseat of the car.

"I could use someone like you to do some of the yard work my husband never gets around to. He travels a lot," she was saying with a slow smile.

"Jason's pretty busy here at the store," said Ted briskly. A lot of housewives seemed to flip out sexually at the grocery store. Maybe burly box boys and checkers with nice smiles were the only men they saw besides their apparently deficient husbands. Ted had seen enough in his time to get pretty cynical.

"Come on, Jason," he said. "Let's take a break out by the loading dock."

"Okay," said Jason, wheeling the customer's empty cart back.

He jammed it into the row outside the door, and the two of them walked around to the back of the store. It was really the only place anyone had any privacy.

"I'm worried about you," said Ted, as the two of them leaned against the wall. "Tell me what you told the cops."

106

Jason took a deep breath. "I feel better now I told them," he said. "I wanted to tell you but I thought I'd get in trouble. They seemed to know I had something to tell them."

No kidding, thought Ted. After all, Jason had been weeping, trembling, and looking generally agitated and on the brink of some terrible outburst. The kid had absolutely no guile.

"You followed Ginger home?" prompted Ted.

"Yeah. It was a really stupid thing to do. She was just so pretty and soft and shiny, and she smiled at me so nice. I wanted to see where she lived. I thought maybe I'd have a chance to talk to her somehow. I hadn't figured that part out yet. But I just wanted to be near her. I parked across the street from her house."

"Yeah?"

And then some guy came by and rang her doorbell. I wondered who it was. Then the cops came. Sort of sneaking up on me. Two guys in a cop car. I tore out of there, but they turned on their lights about a block away and pulled me over. They asked to see my license and said they had a complaint of a suspicious character in the neighborhood."

"And you were just sitting in the car?" said Ted.

"That's right. The police asked me what I'd been doing and I said I'd just been sitting there thinking, and they said I should go home. So I did."

Ted nodded thoughtfully. "So you were seen outside her place. But no one's put you near her when she was killed. That was a week later. All they've established is that you were nuts enough to hang out outside her place."

"It was pretty stupid," said Jason. "It's kind of hard to explain."

"So who was the guy?" Late at night after the engagement party seemed an odd time for a casual killer. Ted wondered if Ginger had been two-timing the old man.

"I don't know. I could tell by the way he walked and stuff

that he was like in his twenties maybe. Tall, medium, light hair."

"If the police hassle you some more," said Ted, "let me know." Jason might need a lawyer to smooth things over. The kid was such a bundle of nerves that he acted guilty when he wasn't. At least Ted assumed he wasn't. "You get too emotional, Jason. You don't need to fall apart over this. Now you've made a clean breast of everything, try to relax."

"Yeah, I know," said Jason.

Ted looked at Jason's young and foolish face and sighed. "What did you follow her home for anyway?" he said. "You can't do stuff like that. There's too many crazy guys around. Women are afraid all the time. They read this stuff in *People* magazine about movie stars being stalked and all that. You have to be careful."

"I thought I loved her," said Jason simply.

Ted snorted.

"I did. She was so beautiful."

"She was old enough to be your mother, she was engaged to Mr. Krogstad, and you met her for thirty seconds. That's not love."

"I never felt like that before," said Jason, his brow furrowing in confusion. "Like I just got hit hard in the gut, you know?"

"Yeah," said Ted, who recalled stumbling around in a red-hot sexual fog when he was seventeen. "I guess so. But dammit, Jason, don't follow old broads around at night. Find some nice girl at school or at a mall and ask her out to the movies or something, and let nature take its course." Ted shook his head. The kid was all mixed up.

"Gee, I don't know," mumbled Jason.

"They'll need you back at the front end," said Ted brusquely.

"Yeah. Okay." Jason loped off back around the building and Ted sighed, then went in through the rear doors to the back of the store.

108

He walked past Leonard LeBlanc's corner office quickly, hoping Leonard wouldn't notice him and engage him in conversation. They'd installed Leonard in a distant office with a door because he drove the meat guys nuts, but Leonard always left it open in the vain hope someone would drop by.

Ted was surprised to hear voices coming out of Leonard's office, so he unconsciously slowed down and cast his eyes to the side. He was surprised to see the two detectives standing there. Leonard was explaining how his lobster holding tank worked.

"A lot of people wonder why we put rubber bands on their claws," he was saying. "The truth is, the little guys, left alone, cannibalize each other." He chuckled fondly.

"You sure got a lot of them in there," said MacNab. The lobsters were indeed stacked up like cordwood. It was only the tank in the display area, under the gaze of the customers, where they were really free to scuttle around the bottom. Ted noticed MacNab was stepping backwards as if trying to make a polite retreat.

"Live tanks are going to be where it's at," said Leonard with a gleam in his eye. "You'll see all kinds of things swimming around. We're light-years behind in this country, seafood-wise. Why, we don't even have a decent inspection system. You have to rely on a well-educated seafood buyer at the retail level."

"Is that so?" said Lukowski.

"Yeah, we'll keep it in mind," said MacNab.

Leonard didn't see the detective roll his eyes at Lukowski, because Leonard had removed his glasses and was polishing them. The gesture reminded Ted of the optician, Mr. Wyatt, and what had seemed so strange on the phone.

"Well, so long," said Lukowski, with an air of hopefulness, tinged with a sort of gloomy resignation that Leonard wouldn't put a lid on it that easily.

Mr. Wyatt, Ted had just realized, seemed rather disappointed that the funeral wasn't Karl Krogstad's funeral. Strange. And strange too that Stan had been running around telling his cronies that Karl had one foot in the grave.

14

Leonard LeBlanc looked up and didn't seem surprised to see the detectives had left and Ted was standing there instead. It probably happened to him all the time. "I was telling them about freezer burn," said Leonard.

"Freezer burn" repeated Ted.

"Unscrupulous wholesalers sell slacked-out product as fresh, and some seafood guys are so dumb they can't even see freezer burn. Ice crystals form in the flesh and expand, breaking down the cell structure."

"I guess they were here asking about the key," said Ted.

"That's right. A key. I told them about those missing crab legs. Think they'll find out who took 'em? It'll screw up

111

my monthly totals. The fact is, a well-run department can be a profit center, and I'm so close to reaching that I can taste it."

"Yeah, well keep up the good work," said Ted. "And write me a memo about those king crab legs." He frowned, vaguely remembering Leonard going on about crab legs earlier. Employee theft was a constant problem, but a big case of crab legs disappearing was pretty major.

"Okay," said Leonard, perking up at the interest Ted had shown in his department. "Say, would you like to read an article in *Seafood Business* about value-added shrimp? They're doing lots of things over in Asia with those black tigers. Shrimp's been a real mover for us lately."

"Glad to hear it," said Ted.

"When you process it right away, near the ponds where it's grown in Thailand or Indonesia," said Leonard, his voice rising with feeling, "you eliminate a lot of black spot."

Ted backed away. "Gotta run, Leonard," he said.

"Seafood is truly a global business," said Leonard, as Ted made his escape. "That's one reason it's so exciting."

"Ted," said the intercom as he pushed through the swinging doors from the gloom of the back into the brightly-lit selling floor. "To video, please, Ted."

When he presented himself in front of Louise's counter, she pushed a check at him. "Will you okay this?" A pathetic ruse. She didn't really need Ted's okay. She had a tight hand on credit here in her department.

Ted scrawled his initials on the check and the customer left. "How was the rest of the funeral?" he said.

Louise shrugged. "Okay, I guess. It was pretty sad. Ginger's mother was pretty cut up, naturally. I guess I never imagined her having a mother. It sounds dumb, I know."

"I know what you mean," said Ted. "It's as if Ginger created herself, isn't it?"

112

Louise looked thoughtful. "She was like a cartoon. Betty Boop. Or Jessica Rabbit maybe."

"Alive, anyway," said Ted with a shudder. "When I saw her body she looked real and flawed."

Louise looked down at the counter. "I almost wish I hadn't been to the funeral," she said. "None of us really liked Ginger. She seemed so silly. But the fact that someone killed her . . . it hadn't really hit me until then."

Ted found himself reaching over the counter and placing his hand on her slim, pale one. He turned the gesture immediately into an avuncular pat. "Everybody's pretty tense," he said, withdrawing his hand.

"And those policemen have been around asking a lot of questions," said Louise. "They're talking to Harry now."

"They talked to me too," said Ted. "They'll talk to a lot of people."

"It makes me nervous, Ted. I'm worried about Harry." Louise reached over the video counter and touched Ted's sleeve. "I want to talk to you about it." There was a suspicious sheen to her big light eyes that looked like tears.

Ted grew immediately wary. Now I'm the family therapist, he thought. It wasn't enough that he was running their store for a little less than $30,000 a year.

"What seems to be the problem?" he asked, trying to sound casual.

"Well, you saw the way Harry went after that shoplifter."

"Yeah. Excessive force." He didn't add that he thought it was a family trait. Ted was always trying to stop the old man from attacking people.

"The police think so too. They heard about that incident. They just asked me all about how Harry felt about Ginger." There was a little catch in her voice. "Ted, I think they think he might have done it."

"That's ridiculous," said Ted. But he wondered if it was ridiculous. "Anyway, the police talked to everyone."

"Yeah, but Harry says they practically accused him."

113

"It must be his imagination," said Ted.

"I know. Harry's real sensitive, but still—"

"Listen," said Ted, trying to sound light, "they're asking all kinds of questions and getting all kinds of answers. It's like they're throwing a lot of mud at the wall to see if any of it sticks." He laughed. "I was just talking to Leonard LeBlanc over in seafood. He gave them a long lecture about seafood today. He was on lobster holding tank practices as they were attempting an escape. Can you imagine? They looked pretty glazed over themselves."

"Yeah, Leonard can clear a room in a minute with that stuff," said Louise, but she didn't look completely distracted.

"Leonard gave them an earful, huh?" It was Lance, who was standing right next to Ted. Ted sighed. He'd managed to waylay Lance, but not for long.

"Yeah," said Ted. "Freezer burn. One of his favorite topics. And wanted them to track down some missing king crab legs."

"I wonder just how effective LeBlanc is?" said Lance. "I think his interpersonal skills are weak."

"Yeah, but he gets along great with fish," said Louise. "Which is what we've hired him to do. He loves his job. Comes in at five to set up. Stays late. Sure he's kind of boring, but so what?" She gave Lance a defiant look. Ted realized that whatever Lance said, Louise would try and knock him down.

"But is he a team player?" mused Lance.

"He doesn't have to be," said Ted, shrugging. "He runs that department pretty much by himself and he manages his budget decently."

"Or were you worrying about how he'd do at the softball game?" said Louise sarcastically.

"I'm interested in the good of the store," said Lance. "The whole operation. And the big picture is made up of all the little people."

Ted didn't like the tone of the conversation. He'd been around long enough to know what underutilized managers did. They started looking for people to fire. It always happened when things were going well, and there wasn't enough for them to do, which was exactly the position Lance was in. Although in his case, it was worse, because Lance was stupid as well as idle. And the most dangerous kind of stupid. Lance thought he was smart.

Now Lance could run around and start documenting Leonard's deficiencies. Leonard would be a good place to start a purge. Nobody cared much about him.

"He's doing a fine job," said Ted decisively. "Did you straighten out those problems up in the office?"

"Yeah. I'll be writing a memo about the T-shirts for the softball tournament," said Lance. "I think we should schedule some practice sessions too. I don't want to lose that game."

"Fine, fine," said Ted, racking his brain for a new project for Lance, before he started his management overview.

"Who cares about a softball game?" said Louise. "We've got an unsolved murder to contend with."

"The police are talking to cousin Harry now," said Lance, flashing Louise a cruel smile. "They asked me if he had a bad temper. I had to tell them he did."

"What?" said Louise, raising her voice indignantly.

"Come on," said Lance with an elaborate shrug. "We all know it. Remember when Grandpa found out about that money. He practically knocked the old man over."

"Shut up," said Louise. "Goddamnit, shut up. And get out of the video department."

"Okay," said Lance, looking around slowly at the displays behind Louise, and running an eye up and down the racks of tapes. "How many square feet are we devoting to this department anyway?"

"Just get out of here," said Louise, who was leaning across the counter belligerently, her hands in fists.

115

"Hey, relax," said Lance with a smirk, before strolling off. "Ted, let me see you up in the office in a sec, will you?"

"Yeah, sure," said Ted.

"I hate him," said Louise simply, exhaling slowly.

"Yeah, yeah," said Ted. "You know, you Krogstads are pretty volatile."

"He's a total jerk, and Grandpa adores him," said Louise. "Poor Harry."

"What was Lance talking about?" said Ted, emboldened by her distraught state. "What money was he talking about?"

Louise sighed. "Back in high school, Harry took a deposit to the bank for Grandpa. It was short five hundred. Grandpa said he stole it. Harry said he didn't. Since then, Lance has been the fair-haired boy."

The phrase "fair-haired boy" reminded Ted of Jason and the description he gave of the visitor to Ginger Jessup's apartment a week before the murder. He realized the description could easily fit Harry. Tall. In his twenties. Light hair. Was it possible he'd seen Harry, but hadn't recognized him in the dark?

"I'm sorry to hear that," said Ted. "That explains how your grandfather treats Harry." He thought of the way Karl had snapped at Harry when Harry had bagged the shoplifter. Some sarcastic remark about thieves.

Louise nodded. "That's right. You know how Grandpa feels about anybody stealing from him."

"Harry's had a lot of problems," she said after a pause. "It wasn't easy for him after my dad died. Mom sort of lost control. He got involved with drugs in high school." She sighed.

Which could well be where that five hundred went, thought Ted.

"Then Mom married Stan and he tried to help. Which only made things worse."

"That reminds me," said Ted. "I just had a conversation

116

with one of Stan's pals from the business owners' association."

Louise sniffed. "Stan doesn't own a business. He just wants to own this one. So he can raid the place for his flaky schemes."

"I thought he was in real estate" said Ted disingenuously. He imagined it had been some time since Stan had scored a listing or made a sale. Real estate was the pits right now, and even if it wasn't, Stan spent all his time at low-grade business meetings, acting like he owned Galaxy Foods.

"He's tried to put together some deals," said Louise. "A tacky apartment complex near the freeway that all fell apart. It's a real mess. All his partners are mad at him because he screwed up on the permits or something."

"Oh, really?" said Ted. "That optician, Wyatt, he wouldn't be one of the partners, would he?"

"Yeah. How did you know? Poor Mom is worried sick."

"Louise," said Ted firmly, "I know it's none of my business, but if your grandfather died, well, does he have a will?"

Louise smiled. "Good question. As far as we know, he doesn't. Everything would go to Uncle Junior and my mom. Unless of course he remarried. Mom's too polite to ask him."

"I guess it wasn't too polite of me to ask," said Ted. He felt himself blushing.

Louise smiled. "You want to, don't you? You want to find out who killed Ginger. I wish you would, because there won't be any peace until someone does find out. Oh, Ted, have dinner with me tonight. We'll talk about it. I need someone smart to talk about it with. And I want them to leave Harry alone."

Ted gazed into her upturned face. She'd managed to turn it up towards his by collapsing onto the counter onto

117

her elbows and tilting her head upwards in a kittenish manner.

"All right," he said irritably, knowing full well he was making a serious mistake, and knowing too that he was powerless to resist. "But only if you stop slouching around and stand up straight and look me in the eye."

With a trace of a smile, she straightened up until she loomed about an inch above him, then squared her shoulders. Ted sighed. She looked, he decided, like a Viking goddess.

"Why don't you come to my place?" he said. "I'm a pretty good cook."

15

◆

Marvella Mortensen, known universally at the store as
"Marvella in Deli," took a deep breath and rang the doorbell, shifting the large casserole in her hand. She'd hadn't
been here for quite a while. Not since Mrs. Krogstad died.
She'd brought over a casserole then, too. A sort of lamb
ragout. She didn't want to bring the same casserole, so this
time she brought cod in a cream sauce with potatoes. A
nice Norwegian dish like her mother used to make. Karl
should appreciate that.

Karl's house was a big pseudo-Colonial, with white pil-
lars and a big green lawn. But still homey. Marvella liked
it a lot. After a long wait, Karl came to the door. He looked
definitely haggard.

119

"Oh, you poor man," she said spontaneously. Then, feeling she'd been too blunt, she added, "I'm so sorry about your loss. I thought you could use this. The instructions for heating it up are Scotch-taped on the bottom."

Karl looked down at the big Pyrex dish.

"That's awfully nice, Marvella," he said wearily. "Come on in."

Marvella was pleased. When she'd brought that lamb ragout, Karl's daughter-in-law Ellen had come to the door, taken the casserole with a sort of a frown, thanked Marvella perfunctorily and promised to return the dish, which she never had. Marvella had taken the precaution, this time, of using one of the store's dishes.

"Oh, I don't want to intrude," she said shyly.

"Come on in," he said gruffly. "Have a drink. No one else bothered. That family of mine just bailed out of the funeral like rats." He stomped into the living room. Marvella trailed after him bearing her cod offering. He glanced at it. "Oh. The kitchen's in there." He gestured. "Stick it in the fridge. What's your poison?"

"Um, you got any Scotch?" said Marvella over her shoulder.

"Sure."

"I'll bring the ice cubes," she said, appraising the kitchen. It was really very nice, with an island in the middle. So handy. The colors were a little grim, though. It needed brightening up.

"Glad you showed up," he hollered into the kitchen as Marvella investigated the curtains, which needed a good wash, and ran an appreciative eye over the appliances. "I hate to drink alone."

Marvella opened the refrigerator. A pathetic bachelor collection of condiments. That silly Ginger hadn't taken proper care of him. She probably didn't even know how. The poor man needed decent food.

120

What Louise probably could use more of, thought Ted, as he stirred the garlic around in the olive oil, was some decent food. She was a little too skinny.

Ted knew what everyone ate. It was a matter of professional interest to him, and Scandinavians, of which there were a great many in Seattle, always had grim collections of food in their shopping carts. They cheaped out when it came to perishables, and seemed to go for everything that was white. Whitefish, potatoes, maybe a rutabaga for color. With a cultural heritage like that, the stuff Louise picked up to take home with her wasn't too surprising. Yogurt and cookies. Faded deli sandwiches to eat in front of her videos. No real food. She just didn't get it.

He pulled the cork from a bottle of wine. She wouldn't be here for a while, but he wanted to let it breathe. It was a nice robust red. He was glad she had to work late tonight. The sauce needed a couple of hours at least. As soon as she got here he'd throw together a salad and toss the *mostacelli* in.

When his kitchen duties were over for the present, and the pork was simmering its way off the bone, Ted went into the living room, picked up last night's paper, and straightened a picture on the wall. Maybe he should have grabbed up some flowers.

Suddenly, bells went off in his head. A fear gripped his heart. What the hell was he doing? Trapped alone with her in his apartment. A good bottle of wine. A good meal, which Ted, confident as he was in the power of decently prepared food, just knew would turn her to putty with gratitude in his hands.

Those long, pale limbs, that long, lanky body, and that cute nose. And she'd been practically throwing herself at him for weeks.

He took a deep breath. He may as well polish up his

résumé and trot over to Price Crusher across the street immediately. And all because he'd let himself get carried away. There were a million lonely women in the world. Why couldn't he keep his hands off one of the Krogstads? Not that he had his hands on her yet, but he wanted to.

He tried to calm down. After all, they were supposed to talk about who killed Ginger. That's why she was coming.

He sat down heavily on the sofa. The sofa on which he hoped to stretch out on top of Louise, he had to admit it to himself, and slowly, tenderly . . . he stopped himself.

Talking about the case was even worse than putting major moves on Louise, who might, even though she'd been coming on to him so blatantly, in the perverse way of women, pull back and make him feel like a drooling fiend. After all, talking about the case meant running down her list of relatives as possible suspects. It wasn't pretty.

Maybe he should say he'd ruined dinner and they had to go out. He thought about this for a while, while plumping up a pillow and setting it at the opposite end of a sofa. They could go to a well-lit, unromantic restaurant, and he could be noncommittal about which of her relatives might have strangled Ginger. Because, the truth was, he thought one of them just might have.

The phone rang. He answered it with a frown.

"Ted, this is Louise. I'm really sorry, but I can't make it," she said. "Marvella in Deli called. She was over at Grandpa's house. He's had a heart attack."

"Oh, no," said Ted.

"If she hadn't been there, he might have died," said Louise. "But apparently he's okay. Mom and I are heading out for the hospital now."

"Gosh," said Ted. "I'm really sorry."

Louise said good-bye hastily and hung up.

Ted wasn't too surprised about the heart attack. He'd been expecting something like this for a while. What did surprise him was his own reaction to the phone call. He'd just been planning to weasel out of an intimate dinner with Louise. Then, when she canceled, he'd felt crushed. That sinking elevator feeling. "Damn," he said to himself. "Damn, damn, damn. I must be in love. I hate being in love."

16

◆

Lukowski had never given grocery ads much thought. If pressed, he might have been able to say that there was one day a week when the paper had a lot of them. MacNab would have been able to name the day. Wednesday. His wife looked forward to the Wednesday grocery ads, clipping out coupons and commenting on the items. "Some nice buys on lamb," she would say. "How does that sound?"

Both men were a little startled to see all the effort that went into those grocery ads. They had pulled up outside of United Independent Grocers, a vast complex south of town with warehouses, a fleet of big trucks with the UIG logo on

125

one side, and a sprawling two-story brick-and-glass building of offices.

Inside, they had encountered an officious receptionist who wanted them to sign in and tried to press on them plastic-encased visitor badges on alligator clips.

"Never mind that," MacNab had said, flashing his heavy chromed police shield. "We got our own badges."

They were directed to the advertising department, and made their way past rows of fabric-covered cubicles to a set of walnut double doors. The advertising department had its own quiet reception area with copies of *Advertising Age* and a stiff arrangement of silk flowers on the coffee table.

Beyond that, on the way to Mel Redfern's office, was a large bull pen of a room, swarming with mostly female workers, some of whom wore blue smocks. The women seemed to be rushing around with folders, or, arms extended, big flapping layouts of grocery ads. Along the windows, other workers sat in front of computer screens or stood at easels. The overall impression was one of relentless activity and deadlines.

Mel's office door was imposing, with his name and title, Creative Director, in three-dimensional white letters. Inside, however, the office proved to be small, and crammed full of black poster board and glossy art books. In one corner, pinned to a bulletin board, hung a trio of grocery ads. SAVE A BUNCH it said under a bunch of broccoli. STALK BIG SAVINGS was illustrated by a bunch of celery. The third ad, depicting two heads of lettuce, said HEADS WILL ROLL.

Wedged behind his desk and next to his computer table, Mel rose and extended a hand. "Welcome, gentlemen" he said affably, indicating two small fabric-covered chairs in the corner. "What do you think?" he said indicating the grocery layouts. "Is 'heads will roll' too subtle? Maybe 'head into savings' is better on the lettuce."

MacNab shrugged and came straight to the point. "We understand you own a 1989 Camaro," he said.

126

Mel Redfern slicked back his hair and looked panic-struck. "What?" he said.

"You own a 1989 Camaro," said Lukowski.

"I thought you were here about poor Ginger," said Mel, his tongue, pale pink and pointed, darting out to moisten his lower lip.

"We are," said Lukowski, who wished MacNab hadn't jumped in right away with the car. "And one of the frequent visitors at her home drove a car like yours."

Mel nodded warily. "Yes, I've been to her house. Conferences and so forth. It's a real zoo around here. Sometimes when we put together a TV spot we'd meet at her place to go over the script and so forth."

"I see," said Lukowski blandly.

"So you knew Ginger fairly well," said MacNab helpfully.

"Well, professionally, of course. She had been the talent on the Galaxy Foods account for quite a while."

"Know any reason anyone would want to kill her?" said Lukowski.

"She was a very sweet person," said Mel. "I can't imagine who would want to hurt her."

"Did you know she was engaged to marry Karl Krogstad?" said Lukowski gently.

"No. Well, yes. But not at first."

"Mmm," said MacNab, drawing his brows together. The two detectives sat silently for a moment.

"She didn't mention it?" said Lukowski.

"Not really. She said she liked older men. Was drawn to them."

"You think maybe she was trying to give you a hint?" said MacNab.

"I don't know. I guess we weren't that close."

"Funny you should bring that up," said MacNab. "Because we had the impression you were very close."

"What do you mean?" said Mel. "She was a very sweet person. I liked her a lot." He seemed to regain some of his composure, and leaned back in his chair, folding his hands in front of him on the desk. "I suppose people might have thought there was something more between us."

"Well, it wouldn't be surprising," said Lukowski. "You worked closely together and all that."

"Would you say Karl Krogstad was the jealous type?" said MacNab. "Do you think if he thought Ginger was involved with someone else he'd lose it? Maybe lash out at her?"

Mel thought about this for a moment. "Maybe so," he said slowly.

"I understand he lashed out at you. For saying something about her."

Mel shot upright in his chair. "What do you mean?"

"A little crack about a cup of coffee and a . . ."

"Yeah, yeah." Mel cut him off. "It was a stupid remark."

"Set off Mr. Krogstad, didn't it?" said Lukowski.

"Yeah, he's pretty volatile."

"Tough for you," said MacNab. "He must be a fairly important client."

"Well," said Mel, "we do the ads for a lot of stores. All our stores are independently owned, but to be competitive with the chains they have to band together. They purchase together out of our warehouse, which they all own. And they use a collective ad department. About thirty of those independents are Galaxy stores. Krogstad just owns one."

Lukowski looked thoughtful. "Seems a strange thing for you to say about Ginger Jessup at that meeting," he said. "Her being such a sweet person and all."

Mel sighed. "Look, to be perfectly honest, these grocers are a pain in the neck. They don't understand the creative process at all. Working with them takes a lot of patience and savvy. You gotta act like one of the boys, you know what I mean?"

He frowned. "Who told you about that? Lance, I bet."

"But of course, you didn't know that Krogstad was going to marry Ginger?" continued Lukowski.

128

"No." Mel snorted. "Who would have thought it? An old guy like that? Ginger was . . ." he groped for the phrase. "At her peak."

"You would have thought she'd be with a younger man," said Lukowski, nodding, although there was no reason for him to think any such thing.

"Women have been known to go after the big bucks," said MacNab, with a gesture of resignation.

"Do you really think Krogstad could have done it?" said Mel. "God, that's horrible." He turned a little pale.

"Trouble is," said MacNab smoothly, "to make it fit, we'd have to find out if Ginger gave him any reason to be jealous."

The detectives fell silent again. Mel's brow furrowed in thought.

"All right," he said. "I guess I better tell you."

MacNab and Lukowski blinked silently, as if challenging him to come up with anything interesting.

"We were—uh—lovers. We were crazy about each other. We saw each other a couple of times a week."

"How long had this been going on?" said Lukowski.

"About six months."

"So you were dating on a regular basis?"

"Not dating, exactly. I mean, we didn't want to be seen around town together." Mel continued to hem and haw and the detectives didn't bother to alleviate his discomfort with sympathetic or understanding expressions. "It was sort of a conflict—well, people might think—UIG is a conservative company. I was negotiating a contract with her and so forth, and it wouldn't have looked professional." Mel coughed. "Although, of course, we were very professional. I mean our personal feelings for each other never entered into any business relationship."

"Naturally," said Lukowski solemnly.

"Anyway, Ginger was very discreet. She said it was better

129

if we didn't go out in public. She was a celebrity, after all. She cared about her privacy."

"And you had no idea that she was seeing Krogstad too?" said MacNab.

"Not really." Mel looked rather hurt. "I guess the poor kid didn't know how to break it to me."

"But you found out at that meeting," said Lukowski. "After you made that, er, flippant remark."

Mel blushed. "I was just trying to let Krogstad know I was one of the boys."

"You must have been surprised," said MacNab, "when you found out he and Ginger were an item."

"I didn't believe it," said Mel flatly. "I thought the old guy was hallucinating."

"Did you have a chance to talk it over with Ginger?"

"Sure I did. I called her as soon as the meeting was over. As soon as I got back here."

"And what did she say."

"She said," Mel swallowed hard, "that she was sorry. She'd meant to tell me but things had just happened so fast. She said she cared about me but that she didn't think we had a real future together. She didn't think I was ready for a commitment or anything."

"I see," said Lukowski. "And did that sort of sum up your relationship?"

"I guess so," said Mel casually. "I mean, she was a lot of laughs, but I sure hadn't thought about marrying her."

"So you left things with her on a friendly basis," said MacNab. "No hard feelings. Right?"

"Absolutely," said Mel, waving a hand in the air. "I was sorry, of course, but I understood. Ginger needed security. An artistic guy like me, I mean she thought it was wild and exciting, but I guess she couldn't imagine me behind a white picket fence, you know?" After a pause, he said with a puzzled air, "I never imagined she wanted to get married."

"Women often do," said Lukowski. "They want to get married and have children. It happens all the time. Especially when they get into their thirties."

"Ginger was thirty-eight," said Mel sadly. "But she sure took care of herself. She was in terrific shape."

The detectives knew that Ginger had actually been forty-one, but they just nodded.

"Of course," said Mel, "for grocery ads you want a mature woman. Someone who seems to know about shopping, and all that. You don't want some teenage model or anything. You want a real woman."

He gazed out the window onto an unprepossessing view of warehouse loading docks and trucks. "Funny, though. In a lot of ways she was like a little girl. Kind of insecure and helpless, you know?"

The door opened for a moment, and a young woman stood there with a stack of papers. "We got a problem with the Spanish version of the Price Crusher hot sheet for the store in Yakima," she said in an accusing tone. Then she noticed the detectives. "Sorry, I didn't know you were busy."

"It's all right, Janice," said Mel. There was audible relief in his voice, as if he felt more secure having someone familiar in his office while he spoke to the detectives. "These gentlemen are with the Seattle police department. I'm telling them about poor Ginger." Mel looked self-important.

"Oh." Janice glanced over at the two men. Lukowski had the impression of an intelligent woman. He also saw, in her eyes, a troubled but eager sort of look. The look told him that Janice wanted to talk to the detectives herself.

131

17

◆

Ted was on the phone with his Aunt Angela when he heard it. Aunt Angela was trying to fix him up with a nice girl from St. George's parish. "Your mother never says anything, the woman's a saint, but I know she's worried about you not being married," she was saying. "Of course all the Constantinos marry late. Your own father . . ."

"Eeeeeeeek!" It was an absolutely bloodcurdling scream. Ted yelled "gotta go," into the phone and felt his adrenaline rush as he ran towards its source, which seemed to be aisle four—pet food, tea, and coffee.

When he arrived, there was a woman with her hands in her hair, just like someone from a cheap science fiction movie. A baby sat in the cart, staring at its shrieking mother with glassy-eyed fascination. A sack of cat food lay on the floor beside her cart. Ted couldn't help but notice it had split open and little T-shaped fragments of reddish brown had formed a small pile by the tear.

"What is it?" he demanded, then, startled by the loudness of his voice, he repeated his question in calmer tones.

"There," shrieked the woman, pointing to the floor.

At first he saw only a scuttling movement, then he recognized what he was observing as a lobster, its greenish shell relieved by the bright blue of the rubber bands on its claws. The creature was moving to the side of the aisle, as if searching for cover.

Ted swooped down and grabbed it around the thorax. It was cool to the touch.

To his horror, the woman shrieked again. Startled, he dropped the lobster, and looked at her. He saw she was pointing back at the floor and looked down again in the direction of her long index finger. Three more lobsters were advancing toward them.

Hurriedly, he scooped up the lobster he'd dropped, stopping for a second to see if its shell had broken. It hadn't. He headed toward the new arrivals marching inexorably towards him, their feelers wagging, their bound claws sliding across the floor, but he was stopped in his tracks by another loud noise. This wasn't a scream so much as a low moan, and it came from aisle two. Disposable diapers, feminine hygiene, and baby food.

"Just a sec," he blurted to the dark-haired customer, whose baby was beginning to whimper. He ran around the corner and, knowing what to look for now, scanned the shiny linoleum. There were two of them here. And another female customer gazing in horror as her young child, a boy of three or four with a halo of blond curls, squatted down and examined one of the beasts with delight.

"Sorry about this," Ted said, scooping up both lobsters.

He careened around back to aisle four, tossing the crustaceans into an end-aisle display of corn chips. The dark-haired woman was backing her cart out of aisle four now, and the baby was in full wail.

He grabbed up two more of them, then ran back to the corn chips display and dumped them. He didn't think he could hold three at a time. Before he did anything else, he ran to the meat counter and yelled at the butcher behind the counter. "Hit the pager. We've got lobsters running down aisles two and four."

He ran back to aisle three and scooped up the last one, reflecting that on dry land the things looked like giant cockroaches as he heard the sarcastic voice on the intercom. "Lobster roundup in fem hygiene." Damn those butchers. The union made them brazen.

It sounded to Ted's ears rather like a come-on. Sort of like, "Come and check out our fresh-baked chocolate chip cookies, fresh out of the oven, just one ninety-nine a dozen," that brought the customers like lemmings to the fresh bakery. A minute later, he knew he was right.

On aisle four, a half-dozen goggling customers leaned over their carts as frantic store personnel scooped up the last of the lobsters. Or the last of the lobsters that Ted knew about. When he was sure the situation was under control, he pounded over to Leonard LeBlanc's office.

Rather than hanging open in its usual rather pathetic invitation to drop-ins, Leonard's door was shut. It was a metal door, with a rubber strip along the bottom. Ted realized the strip was rather worn and flabby. In fact, as he gazed down at it, he saw another lobster, this one rather smaller than the others, inching its way through.

Furious, he pushed open the door. He was confronted with a tableau that, because of the lobsters moving slowly in counterpoint along the floor, seemed incredibly still. The big holding tank was on its side on the floor, one side shattered, with a triangle of heavy glass pointing upward

135

like an iceberg. From the tank's shattered remains, sprawling on the floor face down, protruded the inert body of Leonard LeBlanc. Ted rushed over to him, knelt down and pulled at his trouser legs. As soon as he did so, he realized Leonard was unconscious. He pulled harder at the dead weight and managed to free Leonard from the tank, then flipped him over onto his back.

As he did so, he realized it was probably the wrong thing to do. If his back was injured or something, it might make things worse. But once he saw Leonard's slack mouth and glassy eyes, he knew it didn't make any difference. Leonard was gone forever, and his body, emptied of all life, seemed pointless and devoid of meaning, more useless than one of Leonard's own beloved fish carcasses arranged so prettily on ice out in the display case for the customers to admire.

Ted crossed himself, and then he left the little office and called 911 from the meat department's phone.

A short time later, Leonard's office was full of people, crouching over the body, taking photographs, encasing bits and pieces in plastic bags and carrying them reverently around. Ted thought about the irony of this. Leonard's little office was always empty, except for Leonard, and, once in a while, an eager fish salesman. He glanced up at charts showing fish species and the life cycle of the Pacific salmon.

Lukowski and MacNab were questioning him in the doorway and keeping an eye on the proceedings within at the same time.

"So you came back here because of those escaped lobsters," said Lukowski.

"That's right," said Ted, who felt as if he'd gone over it a half-dozen times already. "What happened to him?"

"He drowned," said MacNab. "In that tank. Maybe someone held him down. I don't think he could have done it to himself. The doctor might tell us more."

"Gosh," said Ted, "I can't imagine who would do this.

136

And to Leonard. I mean, I can't imagine anyone feeling strongly enough about Leonard to hurt him. No one felt strongly about Leonard at all. He was just the seafood guy."

"Yeah," said MacNab with remarkable understatement. "The guy knew a hell of a lot about fish."

Ted felt dizzy, and he leaned against the doorjamb. Gently, Lukowski touched his arm and prodded him back upright. "Gotta preserve the scene," he said.

"Sorry," said Ted. "It's just such a shock."

"You'd think you would have been used to it by now," said MacNab.

Ted wondered if the detective was somehow criticizing him for taking Ginger's murder in stride.

"That was horrible," said Ted. "But she was an outsider. I mean she did those ads for all the Galaxy stores. This is different. Leonard was one of us. He came in every day at five and set the seafood case. And now he's dead."

He realized it all sounded absurd. What he wanted to say, but didn't, because it sounded so corny, was that Leonard's murder touched him in a way Ginger's had not because it had happened in his store to one of his staff members. Ted felt somehow responsible.

18

◆

Once again, the yellow police cordon encircled Galaxy Foods. Once again, Ted found himself outside the store, telling the customers to go home. This time, he didn't bother adding anything about redeeming this week's coupons later. He had a sickening feeling they might not want to come back again anyway. And who could blame them?

A grocery store, Ted felt strongly, should be a happy place. Well-lit, with nice music and gleaming linoleum floors, attractive food piled temptingly high, and aisles full of neatly organized merchandise. Shopping should be a pleasant experience. Ted had devoted a lot of his adult life to making it that way.

139

Tired produce, crabby clerks, a dirty floor—all of these could drive customers away. But dead bodies made these problems into minor irritants. Ted couldn't imagine anything worse. People wanted convenience and familiarity where they shopped. Murder was the ultimate retail bringdown.

Ted went over to the general merchandise aisle and found a felt tip pen. Then he went over to the video department, where Louise was closing the till. She looked pale and shaky.

"Can I have one of those big posters?" he said, pointing to the display behind her. "I'm gonna make a sign."

Louise stood on a small step stool and reached for the latest Spielberg. "Here," she said, handing it to him. "What are you going to say?"

"Closed until further notice," said Ted, sighing. He could hardly put "Closed until removal of corpse and final roundup of escaped lobsters."

"God, isn't it horrible, Ted? Poor Leonard."

"I know." Ted lay the poster out on her counter and squeaked out his message. "How's your grandfather?" Ted had already learned that Karl's attack had been diagnosed as indigestion, brought on by Marvella's casserole and exacerbated by a mild angina episode. Still, the doctor had suggested he take some time off.

"He's fine. Stan says he'll outlive us all. Still, I'm glad he's resting. All this excitement might have been too much for him."

"I guess I'll need another one for the other entrance," Ted said, frowning at the poster. Louise rummaged around under her counter and produced another sheet.

She untied her apron strings. "Did he have any family?"

"I don't know," said Ted. "In fact, I'm kind of shocked by the fact that I don't know much about him at all. Just a nondescript little guy with glasses."

"Who loved seafood," said Louise folding her apron and

140

putting it neatly away. "I don't know what to do right now."

"Just wait for the police to square things away, I guess," said Ted. "Damnit, why don't they do something? They should have found out what happened to Ginger by now."

"I meant I don't know what to do personally right now," she said. "Go home, I guess. The police told me to leave. I could watch a video. But I'm too upset."

"Why don't you help me put up these signs," said Ted, who had had the same unsettled feeling. "Then I'll buy you a drink." She smiled. "Over at Fred's," he added, thinking that having their drink at the unglamorous dive at the end of the mall, the sports bar where Junior often unwound in the middle of the day, made it all seem less like a date or something.

She wrinkled her nose a little when he mentioned Fred's, but he didn't suggest anywhere else. That way they could walk over and avoid the awkwardness of deciding whether or not to take separate cars and following each other and dropping her back in the lot and all that. "I just want to get out of this damn store," added Ted with feeling.

"God, you *are* stressed out," she said. "As far as I've ever been able to tell, normally, you practically live here."

They put up the signs under the scrutiny of two uniformed officers, one at each door, standing at parade rest, and then, giving their names, which were written in the officers' notebooks as they left, they stepped outside.

Immediately, a short, dark-haired woman with too much makeup rushed at them with a microphone. A man in a plaid shirt peered into a video camera over her shoulder. "Can you tell us what's going on in there?" she demanded with a sense of hysterical urgency.

"No," said Ted, hustling Louise along with a protective gesture. Louise put her head down. As they walked away, they heard the woman say, "No one is talking here at Galaxy Foods, site of Seattle's second sensational supermarket slaying."

141

"Watch the mike, Sheila," said the camera operator. "You know you have problem with those *s*'s."

"Okay, let's do it again," said Sheila with a giggle. "What a lot of *s*'s. Thite of Theattle's thecond thenthational thupermarket thlaying," she repeated jokingly, her cameraman gaily responding with "I Tot I Taw A Puddytat."

Louise turned around. "What are you guys laughing at," she said indignantly. "A man is dead in there and you're kidding around. Don't you think that's kind of ghoulish?"

Ted sighed, noticing that the cameraman was refocusing on Louise, and that Sheila had the microphone jabbed at Louise's face and was looking up at her eagerly. He interposed himself between Louise and the camera, just as Louise batted at the microphone.

"We're all upset," he mumbled, as he yanked on Louise's sleeve. He could tell by the look of shock on her face that she realized what she was doing, and he saw her pull herself together, flicking back her hair and turning away. He had to trot to catch up with her, and the TV people were in tow.

"Just keep walking," he said.

"Yeah," she said out of the corner of her mouth like someone from an old gangster film. "Act natural."

They both started to giggle.

"God," said Louise, when it appeared Sheila had given up the chase. "I yelled at her for laughing, and now I'm laughing."

"Just nerves," said Ted.

"Do you think they got me on camera? How embarrassing."

"I doubt it," said Ted. "You're about a foot taller than that sawed-off little reporter, and the guy was frantically trying to make the adjustment when I stepped in. They probably just got Sheila talking to your chest."

Without thinking, he glanced over at Louise's chest as outlined by her green T-shirt, the contours of which he could seldom make out beneath her apron. Simultaneously, he watched her follow his gaze with her eyes, coughed and looked straight ahead. He hated getting caught like that, and it seemed rather unfair, really, when he'd just glanced at the portion of her anatomy that had come up innocently in conversation. He frowned.

"What's the matter?" said Louise.

"What do you mean?" he asked, taking longer strides in an effort to appear businesslike and purposeful and in control.

"You looked at my breasts and then you frowned. What's wrong with 'em?" she said, skipping a little to catch up with him.

God, thought Ted to himself. Now she's making them bounce. He slowed down.

"Sorry," he said. "I was thinking about poor Leonard." That ought to shut her up.

"Yes," she said, sounding hurt. "Leonard."

Now he wondered if he had offended her by thinking of the dead seafood expert when he was checking out her breasts. Women could be so difficult, requiring perpetual reassurance. And no matter what they said, they took everything personally. He supposed a compliment was what was expected, but Ted's usual m.o. required he start with praising a nice outfit or something, then work up to her eyes, instead of starting right in on secondary sex characteristics. Besides, if he said "Great tits, babe," which was indeed his honest assessment, she'd probably deck him.

"Here we are," he said gratefully, as they arrived at Fred's, but as he held the door for her, he noticed she was still pouting. He sighed. "Of course, you're very attractive, Louise, which I'm sure you already know." She gave him a small, self-satisfied smile, which irritated him and endeared her to him at the same time.

Fred's was a grim little spot. According to Washington State law, in order to serve hard liquor you also had to operate a restaurant, and maintain food as a certain per-

143

cent of sales. Fred's served chicken-fried steaks and veal cutlets and overcooked spaghetti to a clientele that Ted imagined consisted of drunks with booze-numbed taste buds, or unwary diners who wandered accidentally off the street.

The real action was in a smoky bar where a row of garish video games and a big television set glowed in the murk. Today, things were pretty quiet. A lone drinker in a crumpled suit sat hunched over a drink at the end of the bar.

Ted and Louise slid into a booth. Ted was vaguely aware of a stickiness on the orange vinyl. The place really was a dive. Louise had been right to wrinkle up her nose.

The waitress, whom Ted and Louise knew because she was a customer at Galaxy Foods—a cheerful, skinny brunette—came over to their table. "Wow," she said. "All anyone's talking about is that fish man. Gosh, isn't it scary?"

"Yes," said Louise.

"Guess what? We've had all these TV people in here. That Sheila what's her name. You know."

"Uh huh," said Ted.

The waitress shook her head. "Until you guys get this straightened out, I'll be shopping over at Price Crusher." She gave them a bright smile. "What can I get for you?"

Ted frowned. Price Crusher. Dirty linoleum. Inexperienced meat cutters. Bad produce. How could anyone seriously consider shopping at Price Crusher? Sure, you saved a few bucks maybe, but the quality!

Louise ordered a white wine and Ted, still frowning, ordered a vodka tonic.

"Did you hear what she said, Louise? Price Crusher!"

"Well, can you blame her?" said Louise. "Until we do something about the situation and find out what happened to Ginger and Leonard, a lot of people are going to feel the same way."

"We?" said Ted. "What can we do?"

144

Louise got a gleam in her eye that made Ted nervous.

"I suppose you think we're supposed to tholve the then-thational thupermarket thlayingth," he said, hoping the levity in his tone would make her see the error of her ways. Louise had a stubborn look about her. He had a feeling she'd press him to help her unmask a vicious killer. He also had a feeling he'd cave in and do whatever she wanted.

"Well, we could give it a try," said Louise.

"You've been watching too many videos," said Ted, gesturing at the television set behind the bar. As he glanced over towards it, he was startled to see a Galaxy Foods ad, featuring Ginger Jessup unconvincingly clad in a tight, Donna Reed–style checked housewife dress.

"The best is what my family deserves," she was saying, holding up a can of green beans. "And the best is at Galaxy Foods."

"They were supposed to pull those ads," said Ted.

"Hey!" said the noisy patron at the bar to no one in particular. "Isn't that the one Junior was screwing?"

Louise's eyes widened. "Hear that?" she said.

"I guess your uncle was gloating here at Fred's," said Ted.

To his amazement, Louise slid out of their booth and went over to the bar, sitting on the stool next to the drunk.

"Got another one of those?" she said silkily, gesturing to the cigarette that dangled from his lip with about an inch of ash trembling on the end of it.

Ted, horrified, went over and took the bar stool next to hers. She gazed at him for a millisecond, as if she didn't know him, then gave him a kick, and shrugged one shoulder signaling him to move along. Ted rolled his eyes. Louise as some sort of female agent disguised as a barfly from some B movie was an embarrassing spectacle.

Ted, who had had the foresight to bring his drink along, sat forward and took a sip, watching Louise and the drunk in the mirror behind the bar. He was a rumpled middle-

145

aged man with the haunted look of a lonely route sales-man.

"So you know that lady in the Galaxy Foods commercials, huh?" said Louise to her new friend. To Ted's horror, she was holding the cigarette this cretinous specimen had offered. Now she put it to her lips, pretending not to notice his fumbling attempts with a lighter.

"Yeah," he said. "There's a guy who comes in here all the time; he was . . ." the man paused delicately. "He went out with her." Apparently thinking this version a little too respectable, he throttled up a notch. "They had a thing going," he leered.

"Wow," said Louise.

"She got killed," said the man. "And I kept thinking, God, that's the one Junior said he was . . . um, seeing."

"A lot of guys brag about stuff that never happened," said Louise. She inhaled deeply, bent back her head and shot a column of blue smoke up at the ceiling. Louise was clearly a practiced smoker. Ted had a vision of her in high school, standing around the parking lot with a lot of other slutty girls, smoking cigarettes and grinding them out with their feet before class.

"Yeah," said the man. "There's a lot of guy talk around." He sneered traitorously at his sex in a pathetic attempt to disassociate himself from it. "Hey, you want a drink?"

Ted caught Louise's eye in the mirror and gave her a severe look, which she answered with a mocking smile.

"White wine," she said.

"Yeah, this character is a grocer. Comes in here a lot. I guess they lead kind of dull lives normally," he said, hailing the bartender.

Ted bristled.

"Yeah, groceries are pretty dull," said Louise, giving Ted a wink in the mirror.

"I travel a lot in my business," said the man. "I'm in floor coverings."

"You mean you install linoleum and stuff?" said Louise. "How interesting." Ted could barely repress a snort.

"No, no." He waved at her impatiently. "I sell at the wholesale level. I travel all over the West. I was in Fresno last week."

"Wow," said Louise.

"And Bakersfield." Louise's wine arrived and he handed over a MasterCard.

"So tell me about this grocer. He was in here bragging about that Ginger Jessup woman?"

"That's right. Said he took her down to L.A. I know that area well. I've got a pretty sizable account in Glendale."

"L.A., huh? Maybe she was auditioning or something. Trying to make the big time."

The man laughed. "Yeah, I bet she has a few casting couch stories to tell."

"I guess it never worked out," said Louise. "She kept on doing those grocery ads."

"My wife hates her in those commercials," said the man. Then, a crafty look came into his eye. "My ex-wife, that is. We're separated."

"So when did Junior, this grocer guy, take her down there?"

"Aw, who knows," said the man impatiently. "His kid was in some kind of a jam down there, so he went to straighten it out, and he got the bright idea of taking this babe along with him. He told us he promised her an appointment with some Hollywood type." The man let out a contemptuous laugh, perhaps because Junior's stratagem had been so transparent.

"Sort of a precasting couch couch," said Louise.

"That's right. You're a pretty smart girl. I guess you been around, huh?" The man chuckled conspiratorially, giving Louise the look of a fellow sophisticate. As a suave little embellishment, he clinked his glass against Louise's.

"So what kind of a jam was his kid in?" said Louise.

147

"Who knows? Some college boy prank." The man gazed at Louise from below eyelids that hung at half-mast. "Had dinner yet?"

Ted rose from his bar stool. "No, but we're about to. Come on, Louise, we'd better go."

"Are you with him?" said the man.

"Kind of," said Louise, sipping her wine.

"Let's all have dinner together," said the man. "They do an okay chicken-fried steak here. Let's have one more drink and get ourselves a bite, how's about it?"

"Sorry," said Louise, feigning reluctance. At least Ted assumed she was feigning.

The man shrugged. "Suit yourselves. But I coulda put it on my expense account." He grinned. "To me," he said to Louise, "you aren't an attractive young woman. You're the Mahoney Brothers Carpet and Tile. That's how I'd put you on my expense account."

"Pretty slick," said Ted, taking Louise's arm, watching her stub out her cigarette and guiding her away.

"Honestly, Louise," said Ted, when they went out into the parking lot. "Did you have to lean all over that creep?"

"He wasn't too creepy," said Louise. "He's probably just lonely. Anyway, can you believe what we found out? And you said we couldn't figure anything out."

"Okay, so Ginger and Junior fooled around. Big surprise."

"And Lance was in some kind of a jam," said Louise. "Where are we having dinner?"

"Certainly not at Fred's," said Ted indignantly. "Chicken-fried steak! Come to my place. I have some left-over *mostacelli.*"

"Okay," said Louise happily.

"I don't see what Junior and Ginger have to do with anything anyway," said Ted.

Louise narrowed her eyes. "We have to see the whole picture. All the personalities, all the emotional entangle-

148

ments. We have to get inside the hearts and minds of everyone at Galaxy Foods."

"I'm not sure all of them have hearts and/or minds," said Ted.

"Anyway, if they'd fooled around and then Ginger was going to marry Grandpa, well, maybe Junior killed her."

"What for? Because she broke his heart? I doubt it."

"We have to go to L.A." said Louise firmly.

"What?"

"You probably have about a million weeks of vacation."

"Actually, I have eight weeks," said Ted. "But why do we have to go to L.A.?"

"To check out that guy's story. Maybe we can prove that Junior and Ginger were shacked up there."

"So?"

"Come on, Ted," said Louise. "Don't you want to find out what kind of a jam Lance was in?"

"Yeah, but don't forget about that cast. He didn't strangle Ginger."

"It all might fit together somehow," said Louise.

Actually, thought Ted to himself, he was dying to find out what kind of a jam Lance had gotten himself into. Having something on Lance Krogstad would give Ted a nice, warm, secure glow.

19

◆

The *mostacelli* would probably taste just fine. It was just a moment's work to nuke it and heat it up, although Ted couldn't help but feel sad that Louise hadn't tasted it fresh.

While she sat at the kitchen table with a glass of red wine, he rubbed a half a clove of garlic inside the salad bowl.

"Poor Leonard," she said. "I just can't imagine what's going on. There must have been some link between him and Ginger."

"Not necessarily," said Ted. "I mean, in the movies there would be, but what if there's just some crazed killer on the loose?"

"Crazed killers are usually consistent," said Louise

151

knowledgeably. "I mean, they go after similar victims." She flicked her hair over her shoulder. "I don't just watch videos, you know. I also read a lot of true crime."

"You mean those grisly books that are always right at the checkstand?"

"That's right. It's interesting. Anyway, take someone like Ted Bundy. He usually went after pretty college girl types with long hair. And always women. It's a sexual thing. In their own wacked-out way, they think they're out on a date or something. Ginger being naked and all, a sexual psychopath was the first thing that came to mind."

"You mean you thought it was some guy that got excited about strangling bouncy redheads."

"That's right," said Louise. "Which is why I didn't think I had a chance of figuring out who did it."

"But now you do?" said Ted, trying not to sound contemptuous as he meticulously tore lettuce.

"Well, why not? After all, if it was a sexual psychopath, it could have been just anyone. A stranger. Someone who kept her prisoner for that week she was missing." She shuddered. "Now I know it has to be someone connected to the store."

"Brilliant," said Ted sarcastically. "I figured it was someone connected with the store all along. They had to know there wouldn't be anyone there that night. They had to get into the store somehow."

Louise looked thoughtful. "I sort of imagined some crazed fan, who stalked her. Then, dumped her body at Galaxy Foods, because after all, she was the Galaxy Foods girl."

"But that theory's out the window now that Leonard's dead," said Ted.

"It has to be the same killer, doesn't it?" said Louise.

Ted frowned. "The odds of two people choosing our store for a murder scene have got to be astronomical."

"Unless someone took advantage of the first murder to

perpetrate the second and make them seem connected," said Louise.

Ted sighed. "It's kind of overwhelming."

"What about Ginger and Leonard? Did they ever have anything to do with each other?" said Louise.

"All I remember is one time hearing that they shot a commercial at the store and she was supposed to hold up a Dungeness crab, and she wouldn't do it, said it was too creepy. Leonard explained to her it was simple, you just held your fingers over its eyes or something, and she just freaked. He was upset that she thought seafood was untouchable." He started in on a little radicchio to add to the salad. "Poor Leonard," he said. "No one ever took him as seriously as he took seafood."

"But someone finally did, didn't they?" said Louise. "Someone took him seriously enough to kill him." She got up and came to his side. "Shall I slice the tomatoes?"

"All right. I'll set the table."

"You know," she said thoughtfuly as she sliced, "a sexual psychopath would have been a lot better."

"Better than what?"

"Than someone at the store."

"I know what you mean." Ted thought of Jason.

"Do you?"

"I guess so."

"I mean I'm afraid it might be someone in my family."

They were both silent for a while as Ted set the table, and then he turned as he realized he wasn't hearing the sound of the knife on the chopping board anymore. Louise was leaning on the counter, her face buried in her hands, her body shuddering.

He heard the first loud sob as he reached her side.

"It'll be okay, Louise," he said, touching her elbow tentatively, then placing a hand on her shoulder.

She reached for him and put her arms around his waist and collapsed on his chest. He smoothed down her hair, and before he realized what he was doing, he kissed her temple. Her hair smelled like baby shampoo. He rocked her back and forth and made soothing noises, and then, because he felt a meltdown coming, he gave her a few brisk pats on the back and disentangled himself from her long white arms.

"I'm sorry," she said, looking red and blotchy.

"You need food," he said firmly. "Eat. Eat. You'll feel better." He became aware, vaguely at first, that he sounded just like his grandmother. *"Mangia, mangia, che ti fa' bene,"* he said with an operatic flourish, gathering up the tomatoes, tossing them dramatically in the salad, and guiding her to the table.

"You're really sweet," she said, smiling a little and using the heel of her hand to erase any possible mascara streaks.

"Oh," he said recklessly, pouring his homemade vinaigrette on the salad, "you're just like all Nordic women. You get excited when I speak Italian."

"Ted," she said earnestly, leaning across the table and looking, he had to admit, appealingly helpless and bright eyed—her lashes thicker and darker looking with tears "Will you help me find out what happened?"

"Of course," he said solemnly. "Of course I will, Louise."

The next day, after the police had mercifully allowed them to reopen, Ted strolled down the cookie and cracker aisle. He wondered how wise he had been to have made such a promise. The chances of his solving a couple of brutal murders in his spare time seemed slim. Would Louise consider him a failure if he didn't come through for her?

Besides, she was worried her own family might be involved. How grateful would she be if that were true and Ted managed somehow to find out? The whole thing was ridiculous. Why did he invite her over to his place in the first

154

place? That was his first stupid mistake. She had left soon after dinner, leaving him feeling confused and unhappy.

Lost in thought as he was, Ted was too slow to avoid Jerry Dugan, a sales rep for Aunt Ethel's cookies. Jerry was bent over his allotted shelf space, jamming packages of cookies onto the shelves, his fat back straining against his polyester sports jacket, which was wrinkled to the shoulder blades.

Ted tried to quicken his pace, but Jerry managed to turn around and catch him. "Ted, my man," he said, pressing forward with a pudgy hand and pumping Ted's hand enthusiastically. Jerry smelled of cheap aftershave, cigarettes, and cookies. "Working hard or hardly working?"

"Where've you been, Jerry?" said Ted coldly. "Your space has been looking pretty crummy. I let the guys on either side of you take a foot, 'cause you haven't been by."

"Yeah, my stuff really moves, doesn't it?" said Jerry. "I don't know why you guys don't loosen up and give me something at eye level so you can see what Aunt Ethel really can do at full bore."

"We've been around and around on that," said Ted.

"Hell, this bottom shelf here'd throw out a midget's back," complained Jerry.

"Yeah, well, we have to allocate space by results."

"You just said I sold out."

"You haven't been here for six weeks," said Ted patiently. "I call your office and the girl says she'll page you."

"Is that so?" said Jerry, looking unconvincingly shocked. He whipped out his pager, jimmied the back off with a dime and peered into the inner workings. "Wonder if these batteries are screwy or what."

"A visual check won't tell you," said Ted.

Jerry slammed the pager against the palm of his hand, as if to magically connect some loose wires. " 'Course I'm out of range a lot. I've got a huge territory to cover. North to Marysville, south to Tacoma, east to the mountains, and west to the ocean. And boy, is this shit moving."

155

A little boy came up to the display and chose some chocolate-covered marshmallows from the shelf above Aunt Ethel's.

"Hey kid," said Jerry sharply. "You don't want that. Try Aunt Ethel's chocolate Dream Delights."

"I don't like them," said the child politely.

Jerry's arm shot out and a fat, hairy hand with a diamond pinkie ring encircled the boy's wrist. "How do you know if you haven't tried 'em," he said menacingly.

"Let go!" said the boy.

"Peter!" said the boy's mother sharply. "Don't talk to strange men." She gave Jerry a look that could kill, and pulled her son protectively back towards her. The boy put his cookies into the cart and gave Jerry a contemptuous but frightened look.

"Little bastard doesn't know jack shit about cookies," muttered Jerry.

"Do me a favor," said Ted through clenched teeth, "when you come in to stock the shelves, which I hope you'll be doing on a more consistent basis from now on, don't talk to my customers."

"A little personal selling never hurt," said Jerry, looking offended. "Listen, I'm glad you're here, 'cause I wanted to talk to you about a killer end-aisle display we've got going. It's a terrific program. I noticed you had those Mexican dinners up there. Hey, it's old, it's stale, forget it. You need new excitement. This display is a real eye-catcher, nine bins, and a beautiful backboard, big portrait of Aunt Ethel, and her eyes kind of follow you like those pictures of Jesus, you know? Everyone loves the old broad. It's a real winner. I got everything out in the car, I can get it up in a few minutes."

"Forget it," said Ted.

"I don't know why you have to be so negative," said Jerry, his voice now taking on a whiny tone. "And while we're at it, how come you don't allocate space for the full nine items

156

in our line? The gingersnaps are dynamite and the Lemon Lovedrops are a big mover for Price Crusher across the street. He does great with 'em. They're a traffic builder. Why, people come to his store just to get 'em 'cause you don't have 'em." Jerry shook his head sadly at Ted's lost business. "You're missing the boat, guy," he said.

"I'll take my chances," said Ted.

Jerry ran a hand over his well-oiled, sparse hair, which consisted of a few long, kluged together strands draped over a pink bald dome in a pathetic attempt to simulate a full head of hair.

"How about giving that display a chance to show you what Aunt Ethel can do," said Jerry. "There's one bin for all nine items and you can see for yourself how well they all move."

"Gee, Jerry," said Ted sarcastically, "how come I spend weeks trying to get you in here and when you finally show up I can't get rid of you?"

"I don't think you're being fair," said Jerry.

"Neither do your competitors," said Ted. "I've had complaints from other vendors. They say you've been chumping them. That melted Fudgsicle in the Nabisco section, that was your work, wasn't it?"

Jerry allowed his eyes to open wide and his mouth to fall open. "Hey, I got a great product line. I don't need to fall back on those old stunts to slow down the competition."

"And one of my clerks spotted you pulverizing the Oreos with a can of beans and franks."

Jerry shrugged. "That's the way the cookie crumbles," he said.

Ted frowned.

"Come on, just a joke. Hey, listen to this one. Salesman says 'I got two orders today. Get out and stay out.' Get it?"

Ted glanced down at Jerry's tie, which left about four shirt buttons exposed above the large Navajo belt buckle. Ted wasn't prejudiced against fat people, but everything about Jerry bugged him. He reflected that standard length ties weren't long enough to accommodate the gut Jerry had developed sitting in his car, ignoring his pager, chain-smoking cigarettes and eating Aunt Ethel's cookies all day.

The tie itself was a nasty magenta-and-turquoise number so garish that Ted found himself laughing out loud.

Jerry, naturally, assumed Ted was laughing at his sallies, and his face broke into a smile. He sidled up to Ted and put an arm around him. "Hey, I knew you had a sense of humor. Why don't I go out and get that display and set her up right now. What do you say?" He gave Ted's shoulder an affectionate squeeze.

"No," said Ted, wriggling from his grasp. "Listen Jerry, don't even ask me for a display until you clean up your act. We have to face your damn shelves for you because you don't show up, and when you do you trash your competitors' products, steal their linear footage, bug the customers, and ask for favors."

"Speaking of favors," said Jerry with a confidential wink, reaching into his inside pocket, "I just happen to have a couple of Sonics tickets. Can you use 'em?"

"No thanks," said Ted.

"Well, here's a package of cookies," said Jerry, pressing some oatmeal thins into Ted's hand. "And how about some of those two-for-one dining out coupons? You can use them all over town."

"No thanks," said Ted.

"What's the matter? Need a date?" Jerry leaned forward with a gleam in his eye. "My sister and her hubby just split up. She's a great-looking gal, and real lonely."

"All I need from you," said Ted patiently, "is a little professionalism. It's real simple. Show up. Keep the shelves stocked and looking good. Keep your fat hands off your competitors' space and act like a gentleman."

"What do you mean act like a gentleman?" demanded Jerry belligerently. "Huh? Tell me?"

158

"Well, maybe you could start by not pimping your own sister for a few packages of cookies," said Ted, exasperated.

Jerry's eyes narrowed, and Ted saw a flicker of real rage on the foolish face. "Look, Jerry, I'm sorry," he began, but Jerry turned away from him, gathered up a few packages of cookies and waddled off amidst the crinkling of cellophane. Ted sighed. Maybe he'd been too hard on Jerry. Things were pretty tense lately.

Just out of idle curiousity, Ted investigated the neat Nabisco display above Jerry's area. Tentatively, he reached back behind the boxes, and felt around. Much to his horror, he encountered something sticky. Tearing away at the boxes, he discovered a pint bottle of maple syrup open and on its side. The syrup was leaking all over the cookie packages. Worst of all, the syrup retailed for over three dollars.

Ted was furious. He went to the front end and paged for someone to clean up the mess, then he went up to the office. He was going to call Aunt Ethel's and tell them either they send another salesman or the line was out of the store. This was ridiculous.

Before he had a chance, though, he had to take a couple of incoming calls, and the whole incident slipped his mind. It wasn't until twenty minutes later, while he was back at the cookie aisle, that he remembered. He strode purposefully back up to the office to make the call.

Much to his horror, he saw Lance and Jerry chatting cozily at his own desk, Lance sitting in Ted's chair and drinking coffee out of Ted's coffee cup. "What's going on here?" he demanded. He glared at Jerry and said to Lance, "We don't let salesmen up here. We keep 'em on the floor where they belong."

"See what I'm up against, Lance," said Jerry, shaking his head sadly.

"We cleaned up the syrup for you," said Ted. "Next time, use corn syrup, not maple syrup. It's cheaper."

159

"Always a kidder," said Jerry, waving his hand and chuckling.

"Yeah," said Lance, looking confused but managing a little guffaw anyway, just to be one of the boys.

"What seems to be the problem?" said Ted, trying to figure out how to oust Lance from his chair and take possession of it once again, so as to have some sort of psychological advantage.

"We're just finishing up," said Jerry. "So long, Lance." He rose, and shook Lance's hand. "Welcome aboard. Nice to see some real selling spirit here at Galaxy."

"Sure thing, Jer," said Lance. He patted his jacket pocket. "And I sure appreciate those Sonics tickets."

"Maybe Lance would like to meet your sister too," said Ted sweetly.

Jerry shot him another look, but Ted was wary. The hate was still there, but there was gloating too.

Ted had a sick, sinking feeling. He didn't want to know, so he didn't ask Lance. He just sidled behind the desk and started opening the desk drawer into Lance's chest so Lance would get the hint and get out of his personal space. Lance got up and sauntered out of the office, as if he owned the place, which Ted reflected, he practically did.

A few minutes later, Ted stood at the window overlooking the selling floor and saw that what he had feared the most had come to pass. At the end of aisle seven, Jerry Dugan, stripped down to his short-sleeved white shirt, was muscling around a couple of big things that looked like trash cans and some unwieldy poles. Nearby, Lance stood in his gray silk suit, smiling.

Ted was furious. By the time he clattered down the stairs and made his way over there, Jerry was standing in the middle of a pile of poles, bins, rolls of corrugated cardboard in garish colors, and a couple of shopping carts full of Aunt Ethel's cookies. To one side stood a pile of jettisoned Mexican dinners and some rolled-up Mexican flags.

160

Jerry was scratching his head and peering at a diagram. "I guess we start with the bins and then build a frame at the back outta these poles," he said dubiously.

"Never assembled one of these yet, huh," said Ted bitterly. "I guess we're the first people dumb enough to give you the go-ahead."

"You guys have a staple gun?" said Jerry.

"No, sorry, we don't" said Ted irritably.

"We must," said Lance.

Ted crossed his arms. "We don't have any masking tape either," he added. "Or a screwdriver. Hammer? Gee, fresh out." He strode over to the shopping carts. "And who said you could use these carts?" He grabbed a few packages of Aunt Ethel's cookies and slammed them down on the ground.

To his fury, Jerry just laughed. Ted knew he was beat.

He turned on his heel and told himself he had to calm down.

"Excuse me," he said. He had to get hold of Junior right away. It was too bad Karl wasn't back yet. They'd worked up an entire promotion, supported by newspaper advertising dollars, with the Fiesta Mexicana rep, a solid guy who'd come up with a solid, thoughtful proposal for the in-store promotion. What would they tell him? And how would they sell all those dinners without the handsome display that included recipe cards and, scheduled for Saturday, a demo lady in a Mexican costume handing out tortillas?

He had to stop Lance. In fact, he thought to himself with grim satisfaction, maybe this was just the smoking gun he'd been waiting for. A careful word with the old man should do the trick. Lance would be exposed for just what he was—a total slimer who didn't know the first thing about the retail food business. A pathetic little sleaze, who'd sell floor space for a couple of basketball tickets. Putty in the hands of the industry's most objectionable salesman.

Ted rued the day he'd ever let Aunt Ethel in the store.

The only way to get rid of the Jerrys in this world—a disgrace to the food business—was to freeze them out. When they stopped selling, the vendors would get the picture.

He stomped up to the office, paged Junior, found he'd slipped out, and stomped back down to the end of aisle seven.

Despite Jerry's unfamiliarity with the display unit, and Lance's general ineffectiveness, the two men had managed to construct a rickety structure, with a huge portrait of heroic proportions featuring a malevolent-looking Aunt Ethel leering over some bins of cookies.

Lance and Jerry were standing back, admiring their handiwork.

"The old babe's listing a little, isn't she," said Ted uncharitably. He gave one of the bins a kick and the whole structure shuddered. "Hey, this isn't stable. You get a cart coming around this aisle at a good clip, and the whole thing will come down like a house of cards."

"Hey," said Lance. "Watch out."

Ted ignored him and peered up at the portrait of Aunt Ethel. There was something very ominous about the way her eyes, narrowed and crafty looking, seemed to follow you. There was also a long gash on her right cheek.

"What's that scar on her cheek?" said Ted. "Looks like she had a rough night." He shook his head in disgust.

"I had a little trouble with a box cutter," said Lance. Slashed her up a little." He indicated his cast. "This thing makes it tough."

"Don't worry," said Jerry. "I'll replace it right away. We got a lot of these displays back at the office."

"I can believe that," said Ted. "Anyway, this one looks terrible."

"I told you, I'll take care of it," said Jerry peevishly.

"I'm still waiting for the day you show up when you say you will," said Ted. He turned to Lance. "Listen, in about two days this display will be trashed, if it hasn't fallen down.

162

It needs regular maintenance. Customers root around in those bins, all the packages will get mixed up, it needs filling. We can't waste valuable footage on a crappy display."

"I'll keep an eye on it," said Lance testily. "Which reminds me, I've wondered about our standards around here myself. Take a look at this." He strode over and pointed at a dazzling pyramid of canned tuna on the next aisle. "There's gaps in it."

Ted sighed. "Of course there are. It's a basic fact of the grocery business that customers won't take an item off a perfect display. You have to leave a couple of gaps, so they don't think they're messing something up."

"Really," said Lance skeptically. "We never covered that at USC. Don't you think they would have covered something like that in the best graduate program in food retailing in the country, if not the world?"

Ted flung up his hands and looked at the ceiling. "Lance, have you talked about this with your dad or your grandfather? We made a commitment to the Fiesta Mexicana people. Their items are running in our ad this week. They paid for it. What are we going to tell them?"

"Tell 'em you changed your mind," said Jerry. "It's your store."

"Yeah," said Lance.

"You're a big help, Jerry," said Ted. "You know what? Cramming this display down our throat will look great on your trip sheet. Your supervisor will be so amazed. He'll come down in person to check it out. And I'll take the opportunity to tell him just what you've pulled here."

"He won't come by to check on me. I'm Polaroiding the display," said Jerry with dignity. "The camera doesn't lie."

Lance cleared his throat. "I've thought this out clearly, Ted," he said with a serious-looking expression that failed to mask his essential vacuousness. "Cookie sales are increasing. People are having kids. Demographics are on our

163

side. Besides," he gave Ted a smirk, "This Mexican thing has peaked. I read about it in *Progressive Grocer.*"

"Got a broken bag here," said Jerry, handing over a package of chocolate cookies to Lance, who rummaged around, extracted one and bit into it thoughtfully.

Ted started to explain the difference between ad support from Fiesta Mexicana versus the benefits to the store of Sonics tickets for Lance or a date with Jerry's sister, but he figured it was no use. Instead, he sneered and said, "I'd stay away from the chocolate if I were you, Lance. You know you have complexion problems. That zit you had is finally clearing up. You wouldn't want to get a new crop."

"Why you—" Lance advanced toward Ted. "You've got a major attitude problem, you know that?"

He gave Ted's chest a push.

"Don't touch me," said Ted, stepping forward so his face was about an inch from Lance's. He smelled chocolate on his breath. "Just don't."

"I'll do whatever I want," said Lance. "It's my goddamn store."

He swung the arm he had in a cast at Ted and thwacked him hard on the shoulder. It was like getting hit with a two-by-four.

"Ow," said Ted, rubbing the shoulder.

Lance's face was screwed up with pain. "I shouldn't have done that," he said. "My arm, jeez." He turned to Jerry. "Can you believe it? This guy's trying to get me to fight with a broken arm."

Ted seized Lance by his shoulders and pushed him firmly into the display, gauging from the list in the structure just where it was weakest.

Jerry, moving quickly for a guy his size, got out of the way, and Lance fell backwards into the bin of Lemon Love-drops. It was while he scrambled to get up again that he pulled the display over. Aunt Ethel teetered from side to side for a second, and then fell smartly to one side. A few of the bins toppled over, sending packages of cookies out into the aisle. An unwitting customer pushed her cart right into the center of the mess, and Lance pulled himself upright with his good arm on the cart, tipping it, and the toddler in the flip-down seat at a perilous angle. The customer screamed as Ted pulled on the cart to get it upright again, pushing Lance's hands off with his shoes.

"I'm so sorry, ma'am," said Ted, straightening the baby back up in its seat.

To Ted's chagrin, Lance was smiling up at him from where he still sat on the floor, surrounded by cookies. "You've gone too far," he said. "Way too far."

20

◆

"This isn't easy. I just thought you should know, that's all."
Lukowski and MacNab sat across from Janice in a coffee
shop near the UIG warehouse. She swirled the dregs of her
coffee gloomily around and peered into the thick white
china mug. Lukowski thought her reluctance to rat on her
boss was rather thinly disguised. After all, she had called
them and set up this meeting.

"Well, we appreciate your talking to us."

"I mean, he might have tried to act casual about it and
everything, but you should have seen him that day."

"This was the day he came back from the ad meeting at
Galaxy Foods," repeated MacNab. They'd just been over all
this.

"That's right. He was pale and sort of trembly." She leaned over the Plastic Wood tabletop. "He was really upset she was going to marry that old man. He pounded the desk and there were little teardrops in the corners of his eyes."

"So you think he was in love with Ginger," said Lukowski, sneaking a look at his wristwatch.

Janice looked absolutely horrified. "He *thought* he was in love with her," she said, as if speaking to an idiot. "But he couldn't have been. Not really. I mean she was so *fake*. He was infatuated maybe, but love? I mean, you couldn't love someone like Ginger. She just manipulated him, and he couldn't see it. I had tried to explain it to him before all this happened, but he didn't get it."

"I see," said Lukowski. "So he confided in you about his feelings for Ginger."

Janice turned her head, gazing through a grimy window at a big mud-splattered UIG truck that squealed to a stop at the red light on the corner. She allowed her shoulders to droop rather dramatically. "Yes," she said. "I tried to tell him she was all wrong for him. Several times, as a matter of fact." She shook her head sadly. "Mel is really very sensitive, but like a lot of artists he has absolutely no insight."

"Let me guess," said MacNab, "After you told your boss Ginger was no good for him, he stopped confiding in you about his love life."

"Yes," said Janice thoughtfully, as if this were somehow strange of Mel. "It was really sad, because we'd been really good friends. At least I'd thought we were good friends. But then a sort of coldness set in. He never talked about her much again—oh, a couple of times he asked me to cover for him when they met." Her mouth set into a rigid little grimace at the memory.

MacNab polished off his coffee and threw a couple of dollars on the table. "Do you think he could have killed Ginger in a jealous rage?" he said casually.

168

"Oh, no," said Janice. "Mel? He wouldn't hurt anyone, not even a spider—or Ginger."

Lukowski sighed. "But you thought you should tell us how cut up he was about her marrying Mr. Krogstad, and how much he loved her anyway."

"How much he *thought* he loved her," corrected Janice.

"Well, thank you," said Lukowski, rising from the table.

"Maybe we'll be close again," she mused. "Now that he can see I was right about Ginger."

Sitting next to Louise in twin-molded plastic chairs in the departure lounge, glancing down in awe at his ticket folder, Ted tried to reconstruct how he had come to be here.

It had all happened so fast. Where were those flashes of compressed-in-time tragedy that generally saved him from stupid moves like this one? Why was it only now, as they were calling for passengers who needed assistance boarding the aircraft and travelers with small children, that his warning vision came to him?

He saw himself tagging along ineffectually after Louise. A Louise nosing around like some brassy girl detective from a cheesy movie, making a fool of herself interrogating desk clerks. Getting lost on the L.A. freeways in some cheap rental car, on a fool's errand.

He imagined her coming back with some smut on Junior and maybe on Lance, flaunting it around, telling everyone he'd helped her spy on her relatives. He figured the Krogstads would rip off his apron and his name badge and throw him out in the parking lot in a matter of minutes. He'd probably end up working at a convenience store somewhere, selling bad coffee, nuking chili dogs, and selling money orders to lowlifes. He'd probably have to begin on the graveyard shift, starting nervously whenever a customer came in and eventually getting blown away by a

169

drug-crazed gunman. It was a high price to pay for mini-mum wage.

Of course, he reasoned, he was probably going to get fired anyway. After pushing Lance into Aunt Ethel, he supposed it was only a matter of time.

He'd told Louise all about it, and she suggested he take some vacation right away. It seemed as good a move as any, even though he supposed he'd have to face the music when he got back. He kind of hoped, in the back of his mind, that the old man would save him.

Karl Krogstad knew what a valuable employee Ted was. Ted even thought recklessly that when it all got aired, the old man would see what a screwup Lance had made over that display. All in all, Ted thought, his only salvation lay in hoping Lance would disgrace himself while Ted was away, and they'd decide not to fire him for assaulting a Krogstad on the selling floor.

With his career very possibly about to hit the skids, how-ever, this was no time to be maxing out his Visa card on a stupid trip like this. And why couldn't they have found a Motel Six somewhere nearby? There was no reason they had to check into the same Hilton hotel near USC that Junior had stayed at last year. (Ted did admire Louise's ingenuity in digging out that information from the travel agent's itinerary in the tax file at the store. She had sur-mised correctly that her uncle had written off his tryst as company business.)

The hotel brought up new perils. Ted had never once checked into a hotel room and surveyed the wide, perfectly made beds, the impersonal, bland art on the walls, the banks of smoothly gliding walnut drawers, all bathed in the dim light of drawn draperies, without thinking about sex.

This feeling would be exacerbated, he knew, by the pres-ence of Louise. She'd made a big deal of casually mention-ing she'd made reservations for two rooms, but was she expecting him to creep down the corridor to her room?

170

Rationally, he was sure Louise had been coming on to him ever since her grandfather's engagement party. It was all so clear. He could see it in the way she moved, in her eyes—that stock challenging smolder she probably practiced in the mirror. But emotionally, he still couldn't quite believe it. Maybe she was just vamping him so he'd help her play detective, just the way she'd smarmed up to that disgusting floor covering man at Fred's.

He looked over at her with irritation. Louise was a girl who watched too many videos for her own good. Life in the grocery business wasn't exciting enough for her, so she had to create a little drama for herself. And he'd let himself get sucked in because he was weak.

"What is it?" she said, with her usual annoying clairvoyance. "You look mad or something."

"I'm just wondering how you got me sucked into this," he said. "It's really not a good idea."

"You got sucked in when you knocked down Lance," she said. "Getting something on him was your only possible move. And getting out of town is a good stalling action."

Ted wouldn't have come up with it on his own, though. After the story of his dustup with Lance got around the store (it took about three minutes) Louise had sidled up to Ted and said "I bet we could figure out what kind of trouble Lance was in down there at USC in no time flat."

When MacNab and Lukowski went to call on Leonard Le-Blanc's old mother, with whom he had lived, they were met at the door by a stout, pleasant-looking middle-aged woman.

She was a cousin of Leonard's and Lukowski was relieved to see that she appeared not to have been close enough to feel deep grief. In fact, she seemed to regard her cousin's death with a kind of grisly relish.

"Unbelievable," she said. "I was stunned. The last per-

171

son you'd expect anything like this to happen to. Leonard was always so quiet. It just goes to show, you never can tell." She rolled her eyes a little to emphasize how mysterious the workings of fate could be, and led them into a living room that looked as if it hadn't been redecorated for a generation. A dusty, boxy davenport in shiny green brocade with fringe, a leather-topped coffee table, a whatnot with a collection of miniature liquor bottles, and a giant wooden television set, topped with a china shepherd and shepherdess, one on either side of a pair of rabbit ears.

"Come on in," she said. "I'll go get Aunt Mildred."

"Thanks," said MacNab.

"But before you do," said Lukowski, "Maybe you could tell us if you'd spoken to him much recently."

"To Leonard?" said his cousin, looking startled at the thought. "We didn't have much in common. He seemed mostly interested in fish, I guess. He just lived here quietly with Aunt Mildred."

"I see," said Lukowski.

She left the room and came in a moment later with an old lady, whom she guided by the elbow. The old lady had a frizzy head of fine white hair and glasses, and she walked slowly, regarding the policemen with polite interest.

"We're very sorry about your son, Ma'am," said MacNab.

The old lady nodded.

"You understand we have to ask some questions," said MacNab.

"All right." She sat down and arranged her dress carefully around her knees.

"Did he talk about work a lot?" said MacNab.

"Oh my, yes," she said. "A great deal."

"Was he worried about the murder at the store? About Ginger Jessup?"

"Yes, he certainly was."

"Did he tell you anything special about it?" continued MacNab.

172

The old lady nodded like a wise old bird.

"What was that, Ma'am?" said Lukowski. "What did Leonard tell you?"

"It's a secret," said Mrs. LeBlanc.

The detectives looked at each other.

"It's time to tell the secret," said Lukowski. "It may help us find out who killed your son."

Mrs. LeBlanc gave a short, harsh laugh of triumph. "I know who killed my son. The Japs did. He never came home from the war."

Leonard's cousin broke in. "No, Aunt Mildred, that was Uncle Charlie. He was your husband. He died in the war."

"That's right," said the old lady. "Guadalcanal."

"We're talking about Leonard," said MacNab. "Your son."

"They sent me a telegram," said Mrs. LeBlanc. "The War Department."

"She's very confused," said her niece. She dropped her voice to almost a whisper. "It's so sad. She managed all right with Leonard here, but now, she'll have to go into a home. Alzheimer's."

The old lady looked at her suspiciously. She turned to the two detectives. "Leonard will be home soon," she said. "He'll explain everything. He'll make me some toast. That's all I want. Leonard usually has fish for dinner."

"Did Leonard tell you anything about what happened at the store? To Ginger Jessup?" said Lukowski, rather desperately.

MacNab gave him a look that said he was crazy.

"It's a secret," she replied.

MacNab leaned over and said very solemnly, "Ma'am, could you tell me who the president of the United States is right now?"

She looked first puzzled, then crafty. "I know, but I promised not to tell," she said. She gave him a self-satisfied little smirk. "It's a secret."

173

"That's what she says when she doesn't know something," said her niece, exasperated. "She won't admit she can't remember." She gave the old lady a frown. "Aunt Mildred always was like that," she said rather vehemently. "She never could admit she didn't know anything."

Mrs. LeBlanc's face assumed a passive, hurt expression and she turned away, blinking slowly. Lukowski got the impression she knew she was being criticized. Her niece didn't seem to care. In fact, she seemed eager to explain the old woman's shortcomings.

"She tries to compensate by writing things down so she won't forget, but she loses the notes and they don't make sense anyway."

"It must be difficult," murmured MacNab.

"You won't get any secrets out of me," snapped Mrs. LeBlanc, turning back to them.

Louise, wearing white shorts and a black T-shirt, lay sprawled out on the aluminum-and-webbing lounger, poolside at the Kappa Kappa Kappa house. One hand curled around a cold bottle of Dos Equis beer. The other she used occasionally to push her sunglasses further up her nose.

Ted sat rather stiffly next to her.

"Anyway," Louise was saying, "it sure is weird his stereo speaker isn't still here. I promised him I'd get it, and he was kind of counting on it, you know."

"Yeah," said the young man next to her. He wore a voluminous tropical print bathing suit, sunglasses with a cord around them, underneath which jutted a bright white nose, lavished with zinc oxide ointment.

"Can you think of anywhere else to look?" said Louise.

"Naw. I mean, like we looked in the storage area, you know."

"Well, I tried, anyway," said Louise. "But I bet he'll be

mad." She paused and sucked on her beer. "Lance can be kind of a jerk sometimes," she continued.

"Fer sher," said the boy.

"Like totally," added Louise in what Ted thought was overkill.

"I remember the time my uncle had to come down and straighten things out," said Louise. "Lance was in some kind of a jam."

"Mmmm" said her informant.

There was a pregnant pause, which Ted finally filled. "Just what kind of jam was he in?"

"I don't remember ezackly," said their informant, tilting his head back to catch rays more effectively.

Ted tried to catch Louise's eye. They may as well get out of here. Sitting around with this moron wasn't his idea of a big time. Louise glanced at him with a little frown.

"Let's go back to the hotel," he said. "Maybe Todd here needs to study or something."

"Naw," said Todd. "We're having a barbecue. You guys wanna stick around? We're throwing some steaks on the grill." He gazed lazily in Louise's direction. "Just some of the guys and our little sisters."

"Little sisters?" said Ted.

"Sorority girls," said Louise.

Ted sighed. It sounded pretty grim. A lot of stupid frat rats and airhead college girls. For this, he'd flown down to L.A. leaving the store in Lance's shaky hands. Thinking of Lance reminded him of that pyramid of canned tuna, and he started getting angry again.

"We have some stuff to do," he said firmly.

"Stuff to do?" said Todd vaguely.

"Aw, come on," said Louise. "It sounds like fun."

Ted expected a gathering with the intellectual ambience of "Gilligan's Island," and he sighed deeply.

Todd's brow furrowed in concentration. After a minute he seemed to have come up with an idea. "Well, if your

175

boyfriend doesn't want to stay, we can get someone else to run you back later."

"Okay," said Louise.

She probably imagined herself as the sweetheart of Sigma Chi, thought Ted. Hadn't she read all those articles on campus rape? Todd and his repulsive fraternity brothers were probably planning to get her drunk—not too tough when you were dealing with a Norwegian, Ted thought grimly. Of course, Louise was a little older than these louts, but not by much. They were probably intrigued with the idea of an older woman.

"So can I help? Maybe make a salad or something?" said Louise cheerfully.

"Naw," said Todd. "The babes do that. We just keep the drinks coming and throw the meat on the grill."

An expression of intelligence flickered over Todd's features briefly. "Hey, that's it," he said. "That's the hassle your cousin got into." He started laughing appreciatively. "He went into a Ralph's store and walked out with a case of prime rib. Took 'em right out of the freezer in the back room."

"You're kidding," said Louise, as if this were no big deal.

"He stole? From a grocery store?" said Ted disapprovingly.

Louise shot him a squelching look.

"Wow," she said, as if she admired Lance's bravado. "How'd he get away with it?"

"He didn't," snickered Todd. "But he had a pretty good scam going. He dressed up like a butcher. He knew all about it 'cause his family's like in the grocery business."

"Yeah," said Louise. Todd had apparently forgotten Lance and Louise were cousins.

"Old Lance says he's sitting on a little gold mine," said Todd. "When he finished school, he said he was set up for life."

176

Ted interrupted. "So Lance just waltzed in there dressed like a butcher?"

"Yeah. And the bitch of it was because the case was worth like mega bucks, it fit into grand larceny or something. It was like heavy shit. His dad came down here and plea-bargained the thing away. It's like totally not on his record." Todd shook his head. "Lance is like a real asshole, but he always lands on his feet, ya know?"

"Yeah," said Ted. "I know."

21

◆

"Jeez," said MacNab, "It's worse than those soap operas my wife tries to explain to me."

"Yeah," said Lukowski. "It's kind of messy, all right."

The two men had compiled the results of all their interviews at the store and at UIG, and put together a chart on a big piece of paper. Lukowski called it the Lust Chart. They were bent over it now. The chart, based on gossip, rumor, and innuendo, and on the observations of the policemen themselves, showed the relationships surrounding Ginger Jessup.

She was in the middle, with lines connecting her to Mel at UIG and Karl Krogstad, her fiancée. A dotted line connected her to Junior.

Mel had a line with an arrow in it coming from Janice. Junior, a similar line coming from his wife Ellen. Next to Karl Krogstad, was a line coming from Marvella, the deli lady. The detectives had it on good authority that Marvella and Karl (who had made a rapid recovery from his attack of indigestion) had been out dancing a couple of times since the funeral, and that Marvella, according to coworkers, had been carrying a torch for her boss for years.

Lukowski took a red felt tip pen. "Okay," he said, "if jealousy is the motive, here's who we've got. All three guys who were fooling around with Ginger."

"We're not sure about Junior," said MacNab. "But his wife thinks she is."

"Anyway, any one of them could have learned about the others and killed her. Except for Junior. He might have killed her just because he wouldn't want his dad to know they'd been fooling around."

"Thin," said MacNab,

"Maybe." Lukowski shrugged. "But that store nets nearly half a million a year. Junior might not want to kiss that good-bye. And he might have to."

"Okay," continued Lukowski, "In the second tier we've got Janice. She's had the hots for Mel for ages. Mel's infatuated with Ginger."

"Yeah, but Ginger was just about to get married to someone other than Mel," said MacNab.

"Okay, it's a long shot, but that Janice girl spooked me. She's kind of a hysteric."

"Definitely squirrelly," agreed MacNab. "Why'd she call us and rat on her boss, anyway?"

"So she could tell us how wrong Ginger was for him, I guess," said Lukowski, shaking his head at the vagaries of human nature.

"Then there's Ellen. She actually assaulted Ginger at that party. She seems like a head case too."

"Yeah, and it's suspicious that she said she was out of

180

town when she wasn't," agreed MacNab. "But I don't believe either of those women did it. Ginger was small, but it's not that easy for a woman to choke someone to death."

"Okay. There's also Marvella."

"I could see her strangling someone better than those other two," said MacNab. "She's a big, strong woman."

"Yeah." Lukowski looked thoughtful. "It's a classic deal. She waited his first wife out, and then when she died the old man takes up with the bimbo. Now the bimbo's out of the way, Marvella actually seems to be making some headway."

"So if anyone actually benefited from Ginger's death, it would be Marvella," said MacNab.

"And here's my favorite guy," said MacNab. He scrawled Jason's name and then drew a line from it to Ginger. "He cared enough to stalk her. The kid's rowing with one oar, I swear to God."

Lukowski tore off another piece of paper. "Now for the Greed Chart," he said. In the center, he wrote the names of Karl and Ginger. In a circle around them, he wrote down the names of all the Krogstads.

"Nice thing about a family owned business," he mused, "the employees always have all the dirt on the family and are eager to share it."

"Okay," said MacNab. "The old guy could kick at any time and leave it all to the bimbo. Leaving all these guys out in the cold. Who looks best here, though?"

"Junior. He could get squeezed out if there was any bad blood between his stepmother and him. And he's apparently been getting a free ride for years. Everyone at the store said he'd have a hell of a time getting a real job after sitting around for years. A boozer too."

"He's on both charts," noted MacNab.

"His wife's a shopaholic," added Lukowski. "But we're really reaching, I think."

"The daughter. No one's said a bad word about her." MacNab tapped Karen Hamilton's name.

181

"Her husband, however," said Lukowski, circling Stan's name, "he's bad news. He's got a balloon payment coming up on that development of his and he may have trouble getting it together."

"Let's go over the grandkids," said MacNab.

"From what we can tell, Lance is the heir apparent right now. And of course he's alibied because of that cast."

MacNab nodded. "Okay, but Harry is a different story. He's got a vicious temper and a chip on his shoulder. He also cares a lot about that business."

"Which is more than anyone could say about Louise," said Lukowski with a smile. "From all anyone can see, all she cares about is chasing Ted, the assistant manager, and watching videos."

"Which gives me a thought," said MacNab. He leaned over and penciled in Ted's name next to Louise. "If the gossip is true, Ted might have a shot at getting into the family. That guy loves his job. He'd love to run his own store."

Lukowski threw down his felt tip pen impatiently. "There's too damn many of them," he said. "And only one is cleared." He looked at Lance's name a little longer. "Remember Ted Bundy?" he said.

"Of course," said MacNab impatiently. Bundy was probably Seattle's most famous murderer.

"Remember that bit he did with the fake cast?"

MacNab nodded. "He used it to get victims to help him carry stuff to his car, but I get your drift. It'd also make a swell alibi, especially when you had two thumb marks on the victim's neck to explain away."

Lukowski reached for the phone. "Let's ask for a copy of his X rays."

"Good idea," said MacNab, holding the Lust and Greed Charts, one in each hand. "Of course," he said, "none of this has anything to do with that seafood character."

Lukowski, preparing to dial, shook his head. "I know,

that's a real bitch. All I can come up with now is . . ." he switched to the voice of a B movie announcer ". . . Revenge of the Killer Lobsters."

"We gotta do better than that," said MacNab.

22

◆

"Okay, so where do you want to go?" The airlines clerk at LAX seemed impatient.

"Seattle," said Ted.

"Vancouver," said Louise. "Come on, I just figured it out."

The clerk rolled her eyes. "You'd better decide right away," she said, "or get back in line."

"Listen," said Louise, clutching Ted's sleeve. "It stands to reason. We've got to check out that alibi."

"I know, I know," said Ted. They'd been over it all on the ride back from the frat house. Lance, it now appeared, had an excellent motive for killing Ginger. She'd been right here in town when his father had cleaned up the mess Lance had gotten himself into. And stealing from a grocery store, impersonating a butcher, it would be enough to turn Karl against his grandson in a minute.

"If he'd turn against Harry for that missing deposit, think how he'd feel about this!" Louise had said.

And then Ted had remembered the odd conversation Lance and Ginger had had at the ill-fated engagement party.

Just as Ginger was leaving, Lance appeared on the sidewalk. He'd said something bland and soothing about his mom having thrown a drink in Ginger's face, and then he'd said "I'm sure we can talk it all out. Get everything out in the open."

Ted thought it was just some California psychobabble. He wouldn't have remembered the conversation at all if Ginger's reply hadn't been so cold, so firm. "There's plenty we can talk about," she had said.

Which, he had explained to Louise, didn't make a whole lot of sense until you knew that Lance and Ginger each had something on the other. Lance knew, presumably, that Ginger had been shacked up with his dad that weekend. But even if he didn't, Ginger might have thought Lance knew. She might have thought that Lance was threatening to expose her fling with his dad to his grandfather, and thereby put the kibosh on the marriage.

"Wow," Louise had said.

"And," he continued "she might have replied with a threat of her own. 'There's plenty we could talk about.' Which Lance could easily interpret as her threat to tell Karl Krogstad about his own little secret."

Louise had seized eagerly on his speculations. She took it as proof positive that Lance had killed Ginger.

"But how?" Ted had asked. "His arm was broken. And why did he wait a week to do it? And who killed Leonard? Lance? Why?"

Louise had insisted they check out of their hotel immediately and fly back north with their new evidence.

"If he has an alibi, we'll just have to break it," she said firmly, sounding like some crusading DA from an old movie.

"Come on, Louise," said Ted, annoyed to find himself thinking of that pristine hotel room, forays to the minibar as they discussed the case, a quick maneuver to the mammoth bed and its expanse of cool sheets, Louise's long legs entangled in his, his hands all over her white skin and her blond hair splayed out over a starched pillowcase, a night of damp, sweaty passion, followed by a nuzzly room service breakfast in bed. After all, if he was going to get fired from Galaxy Foods, as there was still a good chance he might, despite or perhaps even because he'd uncovered Lance's treachery, why did he have to keep his hands off Louise any longer?

"To tell you the truth," he'd said, trying to sound casual, "I don't want to go back to the store right away. Let's go to Disneyland."

"Disneyland!" Louise was shocked. "You're joking. Just when things are getting hot?"

"Okay, we have motive. But we don't have opportunity." Ted had seen a few old detective movies himself. "I haven't been away from the store in years. These palm trees are kind of getting to me."

Now, at the counter, Louise had decided they should go to Vancouver. "Listen," hissed Louise, "I just figured it out. Ted."

"What?"

"Not you, Ted. Ted Bundy. The serial killer. He used a fake cast. We have to go to Whistler, the ski resort where Lance had that cast put on and see if it checks out."

"Think we'll have trouble getting a room without a reservation?" he said. Louise didn't seem to notice he used the singular.

"We'll manage," she said.

Ted turned to the clerk. "Vancouver," he said.

Vancouver, however, was not their final destination. The ski resort of Whistler lay another two and a half hours to the north. Louise, like a driven woman, rushed through the airport to the car rental area.

"Let's call ahead and see if we can get reservations," said Ted.

"We'll call from the road," she said.

Lance pictured a cozy lodge with a fireplace, maybe a couple of brandies. A nice spot to relax after a hard day's travel.

Unfortunately, things ended up differently. After a frustrating round of phone calls, Ted ascertained visiting Whistler without a reservation had been a stupid idea. Much to his horror, they finally ended up in a large stone-and-cedar A-frame lodge, run by a large public utility for its employees. They also rented rooms to nonemployees on a space-available basis.

The place was run like a college dorm of the fifties, with a men's and a women's wing, and Ted spent a sleepless night on a hard, narrow cot under a thin blanket.

By morning, he'd convinced himself that traveling with Louise was hell, and that she was altogether too pushy. From now on, he'd assert himself and run things his way.

At the third doctor's office, Louise strode up to the counter. "I'm here for the Lance Krogstad records," she said smoothly to the receptionist. "Someone already phoned."

Ted, who hated lying and could imagine an embarrassing scene, peeled off and sat down in the reception area. He picked up a magazine and tried to look casual. She'd never pull it off, but he had to admire her bravado.

"Oh yes," said the receptionist. "We got in touch with

the patient and he's agreed to release the records. Just a moment please." She got up and left the desk. "The lady's here from the RCMP," they heard her say from an inner office.

"The RCMP," Louise whispered. "That's the Mounties."

"Great," he whispered back. "They'll get you for impersonating a police officer."

She dismissed his concern with a wave, and Ted started imagining disaster once again, something that happened frequently in Louise's company. In fact, he reflected, he spent more time fantasizing about disaster than about sex when he was with her. In this particular fantasy, both of them ended up in the slammer—separate cells, naturally— begging to call the American consul. They'd be interrogated separately, and Ted would be tempted to dissociate himself entirely from Louise's activities, but then he started feeling guilty at the thought of talking his way out of trouble and leaving her to face Canadian justice, whatever that was like. He wondered if they wore wigs like in England. It would be more chivalrous to try and save her somehow. Maybe indicate fondly that she was a little bit eccentric.

A minute later, the woman came out and handed a folder to Louise, who smiled and looked as if she were about to take off.

Ted jumped to his feet. He didn't want to say too much. The woman might notice they both had American accents. "I'll just take a look," he said, as if she were his assistant.

"We can take a look back at the office," she answered.

"The lady who called said we get a receipt," said the receptionist sweetly but firmly.

Ted decided to let Louise talk her way out of that all by herself. He flipped open the folder and saw a black X-ray film. There was no doubt about it. This was a broken arm all right. It seemed to be broken in two places.

"Nasty," he said.

A bald, older man in a white coat, presumably the doc-

189

tor, came out. Ted guessed he was interested in why the Mounties wanted to see the file. Ted wondered that himself.

"Yes," said the doctor. "A compound fracture."

"A skiing accident, we understand," Louise piped up.

The doctor chuckled. "So the young man said." He held out his hand. "I'm Dr. MacGregor."

Ted remembered that Canadians were more formal and polite. Of course he would introduce himself, and expect them to do the same.

"I'm Sergeant McDonald," said Louise, "and this is my assistant, Mr . . ."

"Smith," said Ted hastily, shaking the doctor's hand.

"Seemed like a nice lad," said the doctor. "Is he in some kind of trouble?"

"Don't you think it was a skiing accident? You sound as if you didn't believe him," said Louise.

Ted skimmed the chart, which consisted of some chicken scratches. He noticed one thing, though. The doctor had set the arm at midnight.

"Night skiing?" Ted asked.

The doctor looked suspicious. "We don't have night skiing here at Whistler. Where are you from?"

Ted decided he'd better beat that impersonating an officer charge immediately.

"Seattle," he said.

"What? You're Americans? I thought you were from the RCMP."

"We never said that," said Ted.

"But they called," said the doctor.

"I'm sorry," said Ted. "There must be some mistake."

The doctor frowned. "Well, who are you exactly? I can't show patient files to just anyone. What's going on here?" He glared at the receptionist, who cringed a little, and gestured at Louise. "She says she's a sergeant? What army, if you don't mind my asking?"

190

"The Salvation Army," blurted out Louise.

Ted wished she'd just shut up. A car had just pulled up outside. A sidelong glance revealed a two-tone car and a trouser leg, navy-blue serge with a yellow stripe, emerging from the vehicle.

"We're sorry there's been a misunderstanding," Ted said, dropping the file on the desk like a hot potato. "Come on, Louise."

He took her hand and tried to drag her out of the office, but she shook free. "Was there anything strange about the young man. How did he seem? Could you describe him? Can we Xerox the information in the file?"

A police officer came into the office. "Thank goodness you're here," said the doctor. "These two people are acting suspiciously. They tried to get me to hand over the file you wanted."

"Oh really?" the officer looked at Ted and Louise with interest.

Ted absolutely refused to lie to a policeman, but he sensed Louise might, so although he volunteered nothing, he answered every question truthfully, drowning her out on more than one occasion.

"So this young lady wants her cousin's medical chart, eh?" said the policeman. "May I see some identification from both of you?"

Laboriously, he copied down their driver's license numbers into a notebook, and asked them for their local address.

"We thought they were the RCMP," explained the receptionist.

"You thought that, I didn't" said the doctor. "I think they've behaved very suspiciously."

The policeman shrugged. "I can't really charge them with anything." He turned to Ted, "but I'll pass along the fact you seem to be carrying on some sort of an investiga-

191

tion at the same time as the Seattle police. They might be interested."

Ted's heart sank. He felt like such a fool. He laughed nervously. "Louise here is pretty determined. When she gets it in her head to do something, there's no stopping her. You know what they say. You can always tell a Norwegian, but you can't tell them much. I just came along to keep her out of trouble."

"Well, you're not doing too well on that score," said the policeman with a frown. "How long will you be in town?"

"Until tomorrow," said Ted, who noticed Louise was glaring at him."

"Good," said the policeman. "Have a nice trip back home."

23

◆

"Absolutely humiliating," said Ted. "I'm not letting you drag me into any more of this kind of stuff again!"

"You were a big help," sneered Louise. " 'I try to keep her out of trouble.' Give me a break."

"Sometimes it's better to come across like an idiot," said Ted. "People aren't threatened. Besides," he added gloomily, "it seems to come naturally."

They were sitting in one of Whistler's half dozen bars, all modern chrome and glass and hardwood floors.

"Tell me again," she said, sipping her white wine and peering over its rim at a group of noisy men at the end of the bar. They were shouting at a televised hockey game.

"Don't let me stop you from making any new friends," he said irritably. "I know you're sorry I talked you out of that Kappa Kappa Kappa barbecue."

"Tell me again," she said, ignoring him.

He sighed. "The chart was there. He definitely broke his arm. He came in at midnight."

"And there's no night skiing here," she said. "So what happened?"

"Probably got in a fight in a bar," said Ted, sipping his Canadian beer appreciatively.

"We'll just have to work all the bars in this town until we find out," she said with grim determination.

"Find out what? His arm is broken. He couldn't have strangled Ginger. If I hadn't had three of these, I'd be ready to drive home right now. It's only about six hours. The idea of another night in that damn youth hostel or whatever it is. . . ."

"I think we're doing a great job. Just look at what we've found out," she said. To his annoyance, she seemed to be smiling and wrinkling up her nose at one of the rowdy guys at the end of the bar. "Another fascinating floor covering salesman?" he said.

"Back off," she said. "We've done a great job, but we're not finished."

"Oh yeah. Great job. 'I'm with the Salvation Army.' " He rolled his eyes.

"We're at least as good as the cops. They had the same idea. Check out Lance's X rays." She paused for a moment. "Why would he lie about breaking his arm skiing?"

"Because he's embarrassed to admit he got in a barroom brawl. Let's face it, whoever broke that arm of his was probably pushed to the wall first."

"And I bet they're still talking about it in this town," said Louise. She slid off the bar stool. "It's a tiny place. I'll see if those guys know anything about it."

"Good luck distracting a bunch of Canadians from a

194

hockey game," said Ted. "Even your charms may not be enough."

She stared at him intently for a moment. "You aren't going to be jealous, are you?"

"What do you mean? What is there to be jealous about?"

"Well, I was kind of hoping that after we get all this solved, maybe you and I—anyway I can't stand it if you're going to be jealous. Anyway, whatever happens, you've been picking on me."

Ted must have looked slightly dumbstruck, because she put one hand on either side of his face and kissed him lightly on the cheek. "Truce?" she said.

He reached for her waist, and wanted to pull her towards him and apologize for sniping at her, but she had already moved down the bar and was wriggling onto a bar stool next to the rowdy hockey fans.

Sighing, Ted picked up his beer and trailed after her.

She glared at him as he approached, so he decided now was as good a time as any to go to the men's room.

When he returned, Louise was deep in animated conversation with a burly blond man in his late twenties. He wore a T-shirt that advertised Labatt's beer and a tractor cap with a Molson's beer logo.

"So where are the rowdy bars in this town?" Louise was saying.

"You looking for trouble?" said her companion.

Great, thought Ted. Now she'll probably start something and I'll be expected to defend her honor with that big lug who's a head taller than I am.

"No," said Louise. "It's just that a friend of mine in Seattle came back to town with a broken arm a couple of weeks ago, and he said it happened on the slopes, but I bet it happened in a fight somewhere."

"Could be," the walking beer billboard said noncommittally. He leaned over to a friend on the other side of him.

"What was Gordon telling us the other week? About that American guy whose arm he broke?"

Louise perked up, and Ted leaned over to hear better.

"Some sicko S and M thing, if you ask me," the young man replied.

The blond man in the Labatt's T-shirt snickered. "It was really weird, eh. Some chowderhead paid this guy—he was a bouncer over at another bar—anyway, he paid him to break his arm."

"Chowderhead?" said Louise.

"That's what we call Americans." He glanced over at Ted. "No offense, eh."

Ted tried to look as if he hadn't heard or didn't care.

"Where's this guy work?" said Louise. "This Gordon character."

The man's face clouded over. "Gordon's dead," he said. "Didn't you hear about that avalanche that got those helicopter skiers? Gordon was one of them. They dug him out of a snowbank yesterday, poor bugger."

Ted wanted to get an early start the next day. He told Louise if she'd just get ready early, he'd do all the driving and she could sleep in the car. It was still dawn as he drove down the highway, the sun filtering pinkishly through the snow-glazed Douglas firs on the side of the road.

He'd been hard on her, he reflected, as he glanced over at her sleeping face. He'd put down all her ideas while he trailed after her, tried to talk her out of her little detection odyssey, but he had to admit they'd found out some interesting things.

Junior and Ginger had had a fling, something that would have sent the old man through the roof. And, Ginger had had something on Lance that would have aborted his chances of running the store and eventually reaping the profits he'd apparently been counting on. And, most curiously, it seemed that Lance had paid someone to break his

196

arm. This was perhaps the most interesting development of all. That broken arm was his alibi.

Unfortunately, the alibi still worked. Ted had seen very clearly the mark of those two thumbs on her throat. Still, what Lance had done was certainly suspicious.

But there were some great big questions. First of all, if Lance had killed her, when had he done it? It stood to reason he did it right after the party. Hadn't Jason seen a tall blond man at Ginger's condominium? Ted had associated Harry with that tall blond man, but Lance was tall and blond too. Ginger hadn't been seen after the party. Not until a week later, when her body appeared at the store.

And the police said, the newspapers said, the TV news said, that she had died within twenty-four hours. So where had she been that week while Lance was getting his arm broken?

Could there have been some horrible mistake at the lab? Ted doubted it. After all, he had been very close to the body. It looked fresh. It didn't even smell. Surely after a week it would have.

The problem of the time of the murder and Lance's alibi aside, if he had managed to kill her somehow, why would he bring the body down to the store? Wouldn't it have been better to take her out to the woods, throw her in a ravine or a river somewhere?

He wished Louise would wake up so they could talk about this. He sighed. Most of all, why would Lance kill Leonard LeBlanc? He had been talking about acing him out of the store in his vague management reshuffle. Was he so crazy he'd kill him? Ted doubted it. Leonard must have figured something out.

Ted pulled over to the side of the road. He'd spotted a sign in a hamburger stand window, FRESH COFFEE TO GO. Coffee sounded good, but he had an ulterior motive. Maybe, if the car stopped, Louise would wake up and they could talk. He parked up against a snowbank and slammed the door hard as he got out into the cold.

His breath hung in the air before him as he made his way across a slightly slippery parking lot. Thank God the car had a good heating system. They only had clothes for California, and they'd been freezing.

What could Leonard have found out? All he cared about was the seafood department. That's all he talked about, at any rate. Ted racked his brain for what Leonard had said the last time he'd seen him. That was the day he'd been talking to the cops. Leonard had been there when Ted first saw the body, too, but he seemed more interested in his missing crab legs.

Ted bought two coffees, picking carefully through his change so he could use up his Canadian coins before he crossed the border, and he put some sugar packets in his pocket for Louise, then set out across the parking lot once again, looking down at his feet so he wouldn't slip.

About a foot and a half from the car, he noticed a curled-up mouse. It looked dead but he nudged it curiously with his toe anyway. It was frozen stiff.

Thoughtfully, he went over to the car, where Louise, now awake, was sitting up and blinking and fluffing up her hair. He knocked on the passenger window, which she lowered, then he handed her the two coffees.

"Hold on a sec," he said. "I found something interesting."

He went back and gently picked up the frozen mouse. Nestling it in the palm of his hand, he held it up for her to see.

She looked at him like he was crazy. "Why are you showing me that?" she said. He set it back down on the ground and got into the car. He was tremendously excited.

"Louise," he said, starting the car, "that mouse was frozen as stiff as a hockey puck."

"Poor little thing," she said.

198

"Think about it, Louise. How long do you think it's been dead?"

"It could have died last night, or it could have been there all winter if it's been cold enough," she said sensibly.

"Exactly," said Ted. He smiled at her in triumph. "He froze her, Louise. Put her back in the freezer, probably in that big case that was labeled king crab. He knew Leonard was saving it for the grand opening. Then, he came up here, had his arm broken, went back down . . ."

"And that's why he put her in the store where anyone could find her right away—just when he had an alibi. She was in the freezer there all the time."

"Exactly," said Ted. "Ginger was, as they say in the seafood business, previously frozen for your convenience—in this case Lance's convenience—and then slacked out."

24

◆

"Well," said Lukowski, surveying Louise and Ted over the Formica table in the interview room. "It's certainly interesting, and we'll look into it."

"But you guys have to stop screwing around with this case," said MacNab. "If you're right, and I'm not saying you are, and you get everything all stirred up, you could make it impossible for this case to be prosecuted properly."

"That's right," said Lukowski. "The public doesn't understand that the chain of evidence has to be maintained at all times. If you'd managed to get those X rays and medical records, for instance, a defense attorney could say you tampered with them before we got them. A judge might throw them out of court."

"Another thing," said MacNab, "don't spread your theories around. Let us check it out first, okay?"

"All right," said Louise somewhat grudgingly.

"But you do think it's possible, don't you?" said Ted, realizing how eager he sounded. He also found himself leaning forward intently. He tried to relax and added, "Leonard was talking about freezer burn to you guys, and Lance knew it because I told him so. He might have thought that Leonard noticed it on the body. In fact, Leonard might have. He would have noticed. It's a discoloration that happens to fish."

MacNab held up his hand. "We'll talk to the lab," he said. "And we'll pursue this lead." He rose, scraping his chair noisily. "Now you guys go back to work and act as if nothing's happened, okay?"

In the hall outside, Louise stamped her foot. "I handed them the case on a platter," she began.

Ted laughed. "More B movie dialogue. Listen, I was the one who handed them the case on a platter, remember?"

"Ted, I'm worried. They didn't seem to think we'd solved the case."

"They've got to prove it," said Ted. "Naturally they'll withhold judgment until then."

"I'm afraid they can't prove it," said Louise gloomily. "After all, Leonard's dead. Ginger's body's buried. Who knows if they can tell if it had been frozen? And that Gordon character who could have testified that Lance asked him to break his arm, he's dead too."

"Let's give the police a chance to prove it," said Ted.

"The suspense will kill me," said Louise.

"I plan to while away the hours trying to save my job," said Ted. The memory of the Aunt Ethel's cookie display debacle came back to him with painful intensity.

"If Lance tries to mess with you, I'll tell Grandpa he stole that meat in California."

"Don't do that," said Ted. "The police want us to keep quiet about everything we found out."

"Well, I can't let you lose your job," said Louise. "You love that job."

◆

"I don't want to lose you. You do a good job." Karl Krogstad had Ted sitting in his inner office. "But Lance feels pretty bad about the whole thing. Do you think you two could patch things up?"

Ted took a deep breath. "I suppose so," he said. There was no point getting into all of it now. If what Ted and Louise suspected was true, Karl would find out soon enough just what kind of a person his grandson Lance was.

"Look Ted," said Karl. "I know I'm prejudiced because he's my grandson, but I happen to think Lance has potential. He's pretty slick. He's family. He cares about the business. Whatever happens, he'll be around. You're going to have to learn to live with him."

"Okay," said Ted. What more could he say? "I've just been down to the police telling them how I think the guy killed your fiancée?"

"And another thing," said Karl, scowling. "We can't have guys duking it out here in the store, in front of the customers. This isn't Dodge City, you know. Step into the back room if you want to have it out."

"I'm not in the habit of using physical violence to settle a dispute," said Ted with dignity.

"Yeah, whatever." Karl waved his hand impatiently. "Just don't hit Lance again. If you do, I'll have to let you go. That's the bottom line."

"I'll do my best," said Ted.

"You know," said Karl gently, "Lance must have picked up a lot at USC. I bet he could teach you something if you'd give him a chance."

Ted managed a grim smile and murmured, "I'm sure Lance knows a lot," before leaving the room.

"About the last hours of Ginger Jessup," he finished under his breath once out the door. How could Karl be so dense? Ted decided that if the police didn't drag Lance away in chains within the next week or so, he would have to start looking for another job. Working for a lush like Junior and a sociopathic killer like Lance was bad enough, but now Karl, whom he had always respected, was acting like his brain had turned to mush. He wondered what it would take to convince the old man that Lance was no good. If the Aunt Ethel cookie display wouldn't do it, nothing would, with the possible exception of a murder conviction.

Ted sighed. A second later, Karl popped his head out of the door. "By the way," he said, "those Fiesta people have been all over me. We gotta give them aisle seven back. Get that ugly cookie display out of there, will you?"

Dr. Malone, a slight, pale woman with thick glasses and blond hair, scraped into an unbecoming chignon in an unsuccesful attempt to make herself look older and more professional, blinked nervously during the phone call.

"No, we don't freeze the body. We just keep it at around forty degrees," she said. "It's routine."

"No, no," said Lukowski. "Was the body frozen, then thawed out before we found it?"

"I don't know," she said.

"Well, could you tell if it had been frozen?"

She thought for a second. "Yes, the cell walls in the blood would show signs of breaking."

"Did they?" said Lukowski. "Do you remember if they did?"

"They may have. I would tend to associate it with decomposition, but if I'd been able to look for it, I could have come up with something."

"Can you find out now?" said Lukowski.

"The body's gone. It's been buried."

"Well, do you have blood and tissue samples? Can they tell you anything?"

"Well, we've got heart, lungs, and liver sitting here. We could get blood from them. Let me get this straight," said Dr. Malone, pushing up her glasses "you think maybe she was frozen postmortem then thawed out? Why?"

"To confuse us as to time of death."

"That would do it, all right," said Dr. Malone. "But there's no way to prove it now. The organs are preserved in a solution, but whether I could determine at this point whether the tissue was frozen at some time in the past is problematic." She sighed. She imagined herself getting chewed to bits on cross.

"Could you have proven it earlier?" said Lukowski.

"Sure I could have. Heck, they run tests like that for salmon derbies. To make sure people don't freeze some big fish and thaw it out on the day of the event. But no one asked me," said Dr. Malone somewhat defensively.

25

◆

Ted didn't wait for a second. First he called in and left a message on Jerry-the-cookie-salesman's voice mail, even though he knew that throwing a bottle out into the ocean with a message in it had a better chance of eliciting a response. "We're taking down that display," he said. "Come and pick up the pieces if you want them."

Then, he marched over to the end of aisle seven and started dismantling the hated display, beginning by wrenching the portrait of Aunt Ethel herself to the ground. Ted took a certain satisfaction in walking all over the old lady's face, already disfigured by the scar left by the box cutter, as he wrestled with the sagging bins of cookie packages and pitched everything into a cart.

It occurred to him to toss everything in the dumpster, but then he thought better of it. He knew he should stack Aunt Ethel and all the spring-loaded poles that held her up out by the loading dock, but he also knew it might be weeks before Jerry came by and picked up his stuff. During which time, Aunt Ethel would be tracking everyone who walked by with her beady little eyes, a hideous reminder of past rancor here at Krogstad's Galaxy Foods.

It would be better, he decided, to store it upstairs above the meat cooler, where they kept old Christmas decorations, crepe paper palm trees from the Hawaiian Days promotion, the tombstones and cardboard skeleton that decorated Bulk Foods barrels of orange-and-black jelly beans during Halloween, and other odds and ends. Besides, he thought with a certain grim satisfaction, if Jerry did ever come to pick up his junk, he'd have to muscle it all through the offices, down a narrow flight of stairs, and all through the store, instead of loading it easily and conveniently into his vehicle out by the loading dock.

Ted didn't ask for any help, partly because he wanted to get rid of the display quickly and without much fanfare in case Lance was around, and partly because he took personal satisfaction in the task. He'd taken the second load up, and was stashing everything untidily in a corner, when he heard voices through the thin Sheetrock that served as the only barrier between this space and the main office. It was Lance's voice and Louise's.

"The whole store's talking about it," Lance was saying. "You and that Ted both taking vacation time at the last minute and leaving town. Everyone knows what you guys are up to."

"Oh Lance," said Louise. "For God's sake."

Ted felt like bursting into the office and punching out Lance, but he took a deep breath and told himself to calm down. He'd promised the old man not to punch out Lance. Instead, he crept closer to the wall so he could hear better.

It was hard to be quiet, because the storage room floor was actually the steel top of the meat locker below and footsteps made a tinny echo in here.

"Your boyfriend's days around here are numbered," said Lance. "He has a major attitude problem."

"He's not my boyfriend," said Louise.

"You mean you aren't fucking him?" said Lance.

Ted made his hands into fists. He was glad that Louise had the good taste not to deny it. Instead she said, "I don't have to take this."

"I suppose you think he's in love with you or something. It didn't occur to you that a guy like that, some box boy who loves mopping up around a grocery store, would love to marry into our family and get a chunk of the action all for himself."

"Shut up, Lance. Just shut up. It's not like that at all."

"Yeah, right. Where did you go?" pressed Lance.

"Never mind," said Louise.

"Don't be coy with me," said Lance. "You went down to my old frat house and asked questions about me. I got a phone call and I heard all about it. What did you find out?"

"Never mind," said Louise in a smug way that Ted assumed would drive Lance nuts.

"I can't have this kind of disloyalty going on around the store," said Lance. "I think it would be better if you quit."

"What!" Louise was mad now. Ted could tell. He hoped she remembered they'd promised the police to keep their theories to themselves.

"You heard me," said Lance. "You don't want me to mention it to Grandpa, do you?"

"You're out of your mind," said Louise.

Ted shifted a little so he could hear better. Not that it was hard to hear Louise, who was approaching shouting level, but Lance was mumbling in a cool, steady way. "I think it would be best," said Lance. "Avoid trouble. I want both of you out of here. Ted's history after he tried to deck me. He

209

was obstructionist anyway, and then when I hear he's running around investigating my activities, well, what am I supposed to do?"

"Don't do anything," said Louise. "Just wait for the police."

Now Lance's voice was louder and sharper. "What do you mean?" he demanded.

"Just that," she said. "Come on, Lance, you don't think you can get away with it, do you?"

"Get away with what?"

"When Grandpa finds out you stole that prime rib down in L. A.," began Louise.

"He won't believe it," said Lance. "There's no record of it. Just your vindictive word. Besides, it was just high spirits."

"Okay, maybe you can talk your way out of that, but do you think he'll blow off the fact you killed his fiancée?" said Louise.

Ted winced. Why couldn't she just shut up?

"Give me a break," said Lance.

"Is that what you said to that bouncer up at Whistler?" taunted Louise. "The police know about that," she said.

"Who told them?" said Lance.

"I told them that, and plenty more," snapped Louise. More B movie dialogue, thought Ted. Still, he admired her nerve.

"What does that prove?" said Lance. "However my arm got broken, it still clears me."

"Don't count on it," said Louise. "I know how you did it, Lance. You froze her, didn't you? After you went to her place after that party, and begged her not to tell about that stolen prime rib and then you got mad and strangled her."

"No one can prove it," said Lance. "It's just a theory."

"Yeah, well maybe they can't. But Grandpa will know and then you're out of here."

"Listen, Louise," said Lance in a whine. "Why do you

210

want to mess in all of this? After all, you stood to lose if he married Ginger too. You should be grateful she's dead. And I can make sure you get yours. But why make a big deal out of this? Why get everyone upset?"

"Because you can't go around killing people in cold blood," said Louise, shocked. "My God, Lance, you must be crazy." There was real fear in her voice. Fear, Ted surmised, not for her own safety, but because she found herself in the presence of someone who could speak so casually about murder.

"Not cold blood," said Lance. "Not cold blood at all. I'm not like that," he said.

"What do you mean?" demanded Louise. Ted couldn't believe how calm she sounded.

Lance shocked Ted by sobbing a little. "She made me so mad. She laughed at me. I just wanted to shake her. I did shake her, and then I was just so mad—it was an accident."

"Turn yourself in, Lance," said Louise. "If you tell them it wasn't premeditated, maybe you can get—"

Suddenly, Lance's voice turned cold and hard again. "If you tell anyone, I'll tell them you're crazy. That you've always hated me. That you and Ted tried to frame me. When I get through with you—" Ted wondered if Lance was right. Maybe they had ruined things by running around looking for evidence. What real proof did they have?

"Lance," said Louise firmly, "drop it. You're in big trouble. If you care anything about the family, you'll confess. Get yourself a lawyer first. Maybe something can be worked out. Maybe you can say you went crazy for an instant."

"That won't work, Louise," said Lance. "Because of Leonard." Lance actually seemed to think Louise was on his side and trying to help him. "What'll I tell them about Leonard?"

"You did—you did that too, didn't you?" said Louise.

Lance sounded impatient. "He was running around talk-

211

ing about freezer burn. He saw it on the body, I guess. And then he made a big deal about those stupid crab legs. Louise, I had no choice. He was about to figure it out if he hadn't already."

"You make me sick," said Louise. "Maybe you're crazy, but you make me sick."

"You bitch!" said Lance. Ted waited for a reply but he didn't hear one. Maybe she was just walking away. Ted himself was trembling. What he'd heard had been so shocking. Lance was so blasé, so casual. And so confident no one would stop him. Then he heard a chair fall over.

Horrified, he ran to the door and burst into the office. Lance had his hands around Louise's neck. His face was steady as a rock. He had set his jaw in a determined way and he was slowly squeezing. Louise's face was contorted with pain and a horrifying purple; her hands scratched ineffectually at Lance's. As Ted reached them, her hands fell limply to her side.

Ted seized Lance by the shoulders and pulled him off of her. He caught just a glimpse of Lance's pale, frightened, childish, foolish face, then Lance turned and bolted out the door into the storeroom. Louise fell like a rag doll onto the floor.

Ted knelt at Louise's side. He should have come in sooner, instead of skulking in the back room like that. He was horrified to see two purplish marks on her neck—that same mark of two thumbs. He felt his eyes swimming with tears and he put his ear to Louise's chest. He could hear her heart beating, and he was so happy he heard himself laughing. Sitting up, he propped Louise up in his arms and reached above her for the intercom button. He pressed it down. "Get a doctor up in the office," he said. "Louise is hurt."

Very gently, he embraced her and kissed her forehead.

A raspy voice he didn't recognize came out of her. "Get Lance," she said firmly. "I'll be okay." She was trying to push herself up with one arm. He lifted her up and set her down on the sofa. She frowned and massaged her throat. "Stop him," she said.

"Okay, okay," he said. She was right, he supposed, although he didn't like to leave her. He heard footsteps coming up to the office from downstairs, and he saw Harry come into the room just as he got up, so he imagined Louise would be all right. He went out the door into the storage room. It was dark in there and he felt for the light switch.

He flicked it on, illuminating the room in a harsh light from the bare bulb. Through the jumble of stuff, he saw that the other door to the room, the door that led to the old abandoned catwalk, was open.

Warily, he went through it into the darkness. As soon as he did, he felt Lance right up against him, he smelled his cologne and felt his breath in his face. In the half-light from the open door, he saw Lance's face set in a determined grimace as Lance grabbed him by the arms and shoved him.

Ted threw off the embrace with a sharp motion of both arms, but Lance was back again, grappling with him and huffing and puffing.

"Damnit, just relax, Lance," said Ted, wriggling sideways and giving Lance a forceful shove with one shoulder. Lance fell away again, and then stepped back and swung awkwardly, like some old-fashioned bare-knuckle boxer. Ted ducked and jammed his head hard into Lance's solar plexus. He could tell by the force of the blow and the huge, breathy moan that came out of Lance that he'd knocked the wind out of him. It was pretty easy now to just knock him down. Lance landed against the wall of flimsy ceiling tile, nailed up against a row of two-by-fours.

Ted stood over him, then offered him a hand up. "Come on," he said, "there's no point in any of this."

Lance looked silently up at him, and took his hand, then,

213

showing more strength than he had so far, he pulled Ted down on the floor with him.

Ted felt like he was eight years old again, out on the school playground. He brought his knee up and slammed it hard under Lance's jaw. He heard the collision of teeth. Then, he scrambled up again, panting, and pulled Lance up by the armpits and slammed him against the wall. He slumped down a few inches, and, crouching, lurched toward Ted for a second. The angle was perfect. Ted extended his leg and pushed the flat of his foot forcefully on Lance's chest. The image of his shoe placed in the middle of Lance's immaculate white silk shirt lingered, even as Lance began to fall through the wall of ceiling tile, cracks appearing around him.

He tried to get a handhold on a two-by-four, but the weight of his body carried him right through the wall. He let out a shout of fear, and Ted resisted the temptation to give him a second kick. Instead, he stood there and watched as if it were all happening in slow motion as Lance's feet left the plywood floor and followed his body out of the big ragged hole his body had punched out.

He was still in the air as Ted ran to the hole and looked down. There, he had an aerial view of produce and watched Lance land on his back in a large display of pink grapefruit. Shoppers stood at their carts staring at what had fallen from the ceiling. As if a strand of big yellow beads had snapped, grapefruit displaced by Lance fell into the air and landed, bouncing, in a circle around him.

"Damn," thought Ted, as he scrambled to his feet, raced through the storage room past a knot of people surrounding Louise, and clattered down the stairs. He'd promised the old man he wouldn't lay a finger on Lance, and now he'd kicked him through a wall. The drop must have been thirty feet. Maybe the grapefruit had saved him.

From his perch, staring down through the hole, he heard one shopper say to another "This is it. I'm never shopping

214

here again. They got dead bodies all the time, and now one's falling out of the ceiling."

More disaster ran through Ted's mind as he pushed his way through the crowd of gawkers. Even if he survived the fall, Lance might convince the police or a jury that his confession to Louise, overheard by Ted, was a frame. He heard the voice of a trial attorney in his head. "And you expect us to believe this story of a confession? Isn't it true you hated Lance? Hated him enough to assault him when he was wearing a cast, because of a dispute over some cookies, and later, to try and kill him by throwing him through a wall and down thirty feet onto a concrete floor?"

When he got to Lance's side, he was thrilled to see Lance's eyes were open and he was blinking. He was also whimpering a little. "Jeez, Ted," he said, "I think my arm's broken."

Ted turned away. He assumed the medics who were coming to treat Louise would take care of Lance. He didn't even try to surround the scene with boxes or get the bystanders to shove off. He just headed back for the office where Louise was.

He found her sitting up and smiling at a young Seattle fire department medic. Harry was on one side of her and Karl Krogstad and Marvella in Deli were on the other. "I feel fine, I really do," she said.

Ted cleared his throat. "Umm, there's a guy down in produce who says he's got a broken arm," he said to the medic. "He had a bad fall."

"Slipped on the linoleum?" said the medic, gathering up his equipment.

"Umm, no," said Ted, realizing it would come out soon enough. He looked guiltily at Mr. Krogstad. "He fell about thrity feet and landed in a pile of grapefruit."

"Lance?" said Louise.

"We were, um, grappling on the old catwalk and he fell

215

through the wall. It's just old ceiling tile. I think he'll be okay." He withdrew his glance from Karl Krogstad.

"I'm sorry to hear that," said Krogstad.

"Yeah, well I guess I'll just clear out my desk and leave," said Ted. "The police will have to sort it out."

"No, no, no," said Krogstad. "I mean I'm sorry he didn't land right on the floor. Save the taxpayers the cost of a trial."

"You mean you know that Lance killed Ginger and Leonard?" said Ted. "I heard him admit it to Louise from the storage room. He came right out and admitted both murders, but I was afraid no one would believe us, that we couldn't prove it."

"Everyone heard that confession," said Louise with a raspy little cough. She held her hand out and pointed at the red intercom button. Why do you think I confronted him? I was leaning on this thing on purpose while he was talking. The microphone was right next to him."

"I heard it," said Krogstad. "I was down in deli and I heard it loud and clear. At least fifty people heard it. I'm glad I did. I never would have believed it otherwise." He shook his head sadly, and Marvella patted his hand.

"I didn't know what else to do," said Louise. "It was easier to goad him than I thought. I think he's crazy, I really do."

"My God, Louise," said Ted, "that's brilliant. Like something out of the movies." He lifted up the microphone and looked at it with a smile. "I think we should give a gift certificate to everyone who was down there in produce when Lance landed," he said. "That'll calm them down." Then he depressed the red button. "Clean-up in produce," he said.